HOSPITALITY—HALEY STYLE

"I don't fight for money," Ki said.

"You're gonna fight, or you're gonna die right here," Ollie chimed in.

"Okay. Since you insist. Step back," Ki told Jeb.

Jeb moved back. He unbuckled his gunbelt and handed it to Ollie. "Now you."

Ki removed his scabbard and laid it down on the bar top.

Jessie saw the bowlegged man step up to Jeb. A large Bowie knife came whipping out from behind Kiley's back.

"What the hell gives here?" A broad-shouldered man burst through the batwings. Jessie saw the star pinned to his chest.

"Jist in time, Sheriff Doughty," Ollie called across the room.

"Well," the sheriff said, "I see Jeb there with a blade, the stranger with empty hands. Don't seem like much of a fair fight. I got ten bucks on Jeb. . . ."

DON'T MISS THESE
ALL-ACTION WESTERN SERIES
FROM THE BERKLEY PUBLISHING GROUP

THE GUNSMITH by J. R. Roberts
    Clint Adams was a legend among lawmen, outlaws, and
ladies. They called him . . . the Gunsmith.

LONGARM by Tabor Evans
    The popular long-running series about U.S. Deputy Marshal
Long—his life, his loves, his fight for justice.

LONE STAR by Wesley Ellis
    The blazing adventures of Jessica Starbuck and the martial
arts master, Ki. Over eight million copies in print.

SLOCUM by Jake Logan
    Today's longest-running action western. John Slocum rides
a deadly trail of hot blood and cold steel.

WESLEY ELLIS

LONE STAR

AND THE BRUTUS GANG

JOVE BOOKS, NEW YORK

LONE STAR AND THE BRUTUS GANG

A Jove Book / published by arrangement with
the author

PRINTING HISTORY
Jove edition / March 1993

ISBN: 0-515-11062-0

Jove Books are published by The Berkley Publishing Group,
200 Madison Avenue, New York, New York 10016.
The name "JOVE" and the "J" logo
are trademarks belonging to Jove Publications, Inc.

PRINTED IN THE UNITED STATES OF AMERICA

10 9 8 7 6 5 4 3 2 1

Chapter 1

Jessica Starbuck and Ki spotted the vultures in the distance. The scavenger birds swam their lazy doom circles in the shimmering heat high above the jagged ridges of the barren hills, an ominous black stain against an endless burning blue sky.

Astride his black gelding, Ki sniffed at the parched air. "Smell that, Jessie. There's death beyond those hills."

"Or something dying," she said.

"Yes. Something ... or someone dying," Ki echoed grimly.

A steady hot wind lashed Jessie with air that felt as if it were on fire, across this burning desolation of sand and rock and giant saguaro cactus. Indeed, Jessie caught a faint whiff of death, a coppery taint of blood, as dust devils swirled around her brown mare. Saddle leather creaking, hooves lightly clopping over hard-packed dirt, they forged deeper into the bowels of this hellish land. Jessie checked

1

the sky, squinting against a high noon's sun that blazed over this stretch of baking Arizona desert like a furnace. She heard the rattler of a serpent from somewhere nearby. Her mare whinnied at the eerie tambourinelike sound, but Jessie stroked her mount's neck, calming the horse. This was the devil's wasteland, she thought.

It was the middle of their second day on a journey to a town called Haley. Yesterday morning they had disembarked by train at a railhead in northern Arizona Territory, at a small town named Tempest. There, they had rented their mounts and made a plan to infiltrate Haley, a town about which Jessie had been briefed in reports that had reached the Circle Star ranch in Texas by way of Starbuck minions. The town was owned by a Colorado cattle baron, Max Haley. And Max Haley was a notorious cartel figure named in Jessie's log book, the black book left to her by her father, Alex Starbuck, who had been murdered by the European cabal hell-bent on taking over American businesses, and shoving American politicians and lawmen into their pockets. Rumor had it that Haley had sold his ranch in Colorado and built himself a town deep in the heart of Arizona Territory. Rumors had also reached Jessie's ears that Haley was a dirty, wide-open town rife with gambling and prostitution, run by a small army of vicious outlaws, led by a killer named John Brutus. If that was the case, then Jessie knew Haley could be the most lawless town she and Ki had ever set foot in. Max Haley, she knew, had enough money to buy any badge looking to be tarnished for a few dollars extra. Something warned her they would be completely on their own, and that everyone could prove a potential enemy, badge or no badge.

Jessie felt the sweat run down the back of her neck, matting her coppery-blond hair against her flesh. Her brown Stetson shielded her beautiful face from the sun, the thong snug around her chin. She wore low-heeled black boots made of soft cordovan leather, a white silk blouse, brown denim jacket, and brown denim Levis, which hugged tight her long shapely legs. In her holster she carried her double-action .38-caliber revolver, mounted on its .44 frame; the .38-caliber derringer was tucked behind the square buckle of her wide brown leather belt. She was about business, deadly business. She wanted Max Haley to go down, and she was determined to burn down his dirty town around his corpse.

She looked at Ki, who seemed every bit as grim and determined as she felt. Ki wore a black Stetson, ankle-high black Wellington boots, well-worn black denim jeans, a collarless white cotton shirt, and a leather vest, the pockets of which held his shurikens. There was also a .44 Colt in one of his saddlebags, but one weapon was clearly visible. Tucked inside his black sash, inside his scabbard, Ki carried his *katana,* a samurai sword. It was the first time Jessie could recall Ki ever openly toting the sword when they were riding to take on the cartel. But he also knew they were headed into a potential pit of vipers. Ki was proud of his Japanese heritage, too, and it was as if he were wearing the sword to remind him of his roots, or maybe, she thought, to warn any enemy just how deadly serious he was.

As the stench grew stronger, and as they made their way south, around the base of the hills, Jessie looked again at Ki. She was worried about her bodyguard; she couldn't remember Ki ever being this quiet, this solemn and brooding for so long a spell.

"Ki?"

"Yes."

"You know, you haven't said more than ten words since we left the ranch. Something's bothering you. What?"

Ki seemed to think about something for a moment, his gaze narrowing over his almond eyes, his stare haunted, as if he were catching a fleeting glimpse of the future. "I can answer you with one name. John Brutus. An outlaw who has been hunted all over the country, but never caught, a man who would just as soon kill another man, even a federal marshal, as he would spit. A man who probably has whatever law is in this town quaking in its boots. So, if this town, Haley, is as bad as we were told by your people, then we're in for one helluva fight, Jessie."

Jessie smiled. "Well, if you're worried about my safety, Ki, don't. I'm a big girl, and you know I can take care of myself."

Ki chuckled, but there was no mirth to the sound. "Don't I know it, Jessie, don't I know it. But we're only two . . . and against how many?"

"We've already agreed how we're going to play this. Low-key, scout this town out. No bull-in-a-china-shop routine. I know how you can be, like some raging hurricane. Low-key, remember. *Low-Ki.*"

Jessie's shot at humor seemed to elude Ki.

"That worries me, too, Jessie. We're playing it by ear, taking it as it comes. I don't like it. There's no real set plan."

"You, more than anyone else, Ki, should know you should never plan a damn thing. Rarely does anything work out the way you see it in your head. And, you're right, we'll take it as it comes."

They heard the soft groans of misery then, as they rounded the hills and stared out across another flat stretch of sand and rock. The buzzards were now right overhead.

And they found death on the desert floor.

"Help me . . . W-w-water . . . water . . ."

They found him, stretched out beside the bullet-riddled carcasses of two geldings. Swarms of buzzing flies and red ants teemed over the carcasses, a black-red crawling carpet of feasting invaders. The man, they saw, lay in a pool of his own blood, holding his stomach. He had been gut-shot and left for dead. Jessie and Ki dismounted near the dying man. Jessie grabbed her canteen and squatted over him. Flies were picking at the swollen black-and-purple, blood-caked flesh of his face. He had been severely beaten. As he looked up at Jessie, he grimaced, struggling for words.

"W-water . . . please . . ."

Jessie uncapped her canteen and gently placed the nozzle against the man's lips. He was going to die, she knew, but she felt an overpowering compassion for him and allowed him his last request.

"Easy," Ki told the man, kneeling beside him, next to Jessie. "Drink it easy."

Water spilled down the sides of his mouth as he greedily sucked the water into him against Ki's advice. He didn't look to be any older than twenty to Jessie. He had blond hair and a soft, unlined, smooth-skinned face. He wasn't wearing a holster, and there wasn't a scabbard with rifle, it looked like, on his horse either, but Jessie sensed he wasn't the gunfighting type. He was just a kid. What was he doing out here? she wondered.

"My . . . my sister . . . They took her . . ."

"Who? What happened?" Jessie asked.

"Christine . . . my sister . . . six men . . . They rode up on us . . . demanded water . . . I gave them some . . . then . . . they said they rode with John . . . Brutus . . . kept looking at Christine . . . said they could get me a good price for her in Haley . . . Bastards . . . She's no . . . whore . . ."

Jessie placed a gentle hand on his face. "What's your name?" He coughed up blood. "Easy."

"I'm dyin' . . . I know . . . Joe . . . Larety . . . I would've . . . been twenty-one . . . tomorrow . . . Leave me . . . Help Christine . . ."

"Where did they take your sister, Joe?" Ki asked.

"Hills . . . east . . . 'bout . . . fifteen minutes ago . . ." Blood flecks dribbled over his lips; then his stare went blank as a death rattle rasped out of his throat. His head lolled to the side, eyes staring at nothing. Jessie stood, looking at the hills to the east. Maybe a ten minute ride. She saw the hoofprints in the soil, a lot of hoofprints. Heading east.

Jessie looked at Ki. It didn't have to be said.

They were headed into the viper's nest, for their first taste of the poison of the John Brutus gang.

As they guided their mounts up the low-lying chain of rugged hills, Jessie caught the cruel words hurled their way through the scorched air.

"Ah, she's nice. You gonna suck this good, ya little-suck-bitch filly you. Wished now I hadn't shot yer boyfriend, wished he could see me turn you into a real woman."

Cold rage filled Jessie. She saw Ki's shoulders tense with fury, too. She didn't have to see it to know what was about to happen beyond the rise. She only hoped they weren't too late.

"C'mon, Jody, let's get busy. Pop her sweet; then we gotta get to town. Big John's expectin' us."

Okay, Jessie thought, they were part of the Brutus gang, but John Brutus wasn't with them. She looked at Ki, her jaw set with grim determination.

There was no turning back. Once they topped the rise . . .

They topped the crest of the hill. And Jessie found six big, broad, bearded, grim-faced men at the foot of the hill. One man was unbuckling his gunbelt, his sweaty face twisted with a leer, as he stood over a redheaded girl Jessie judged to be no more than eighteen. Her white blouse and jeans were dirty, but they weren't torn, which told Jessie she and Ki weren't too late. But the sick fun was about to begin. The men were packed tightly together in a shallow bowl at the base of the hill, in the shade. Three of the other saddle scum stood beside their mounts; two of the would-be rapists were astride their horses. All of them had revolvers in holsters tied down to their thighs. Gunslingers. No, Jessie corrected herself, they were vermin, plain and simple. Dirty low-down no-good scum-suckers.

The outlaw looming over the girl, fumbling with his belt buckle, snickered. "Bet she's a virgin, fellers, heh? Boy she was with surely couldn'ta done her no good."

"Just shut up and do what yer gonna do!" one of the other outlaws snarled. "Goddam bad idea to draw cards to see who goes first! Sure you can get hard, Jody? We ain't got all friggin' day."

Jessie draped a hand over the smooth polished peachwood of her .38 Colt. Ki already had his fist wrapped around the hilt of his *katana*. Jessie felt the adrenaline racing through her blood. She knew already how they were going to deal with these cut-throats, knew there was only one way out of there and past them. And that was through them, and over them. Sometimes, she thought, you just have to step on a viper and crush the life out of it, so it doesn't bite ever again. As Jessie and Ki slowly began descending the hill, one of the outlaws looked up.

"Hey, Jody! Put it back in yer pants. We got company."

Jody looked up, startled, then angry. A moment later he had his gunbelt hooked up again. "Shit! I was just feelin' the start of iron hardenin' on me here. Shit! Who the hell are you people?"

"Relax," one of the other cutthroats said. "They ain't nobody."

Jessie and Ki led their mounts onto level ground, keeping hard-eyed vigilance riveted on the gang.

"You wanna git off them mounts?" Jody demanded, his hand moving toward the butt of his revolver. "Now. 'Fore I cut you both down where you sit. I'll shoot a woman soon as I'd shoot a man, don't make a damn bit a diff'rence to me."

"Sure," Ki said, and dismounted, glancing at the double-barreled shotgun on the ground beside Jody. "We don't want any trouble. And I sure wouldn't want to see my lady friend here hurt."

"Lady friend," Jody laughed. "Yeah, whatever you say, pardner. You want, we can take her to Haley with this young stuff here. Damn, but she looks good. Bet we can git top dollar for blondie there. You in, stranger?"

" 'Fraid not," Ki said, clenching his jaw.

Jessie sidled her mare a few feet closer to the gang, the tension in the air so thick she figured she could cut it with a knife. She saw the outlaws sizing her up like a piece of meat, licking their lips. Bastards. Her blood boiled.

Ki moved with measured steps toward Jody.

"Far enough, mister," Jody said.

Jessie knew it was about to erupt. Ki was pushing it, but she was ready for the inevitable, prepared to fight right beside her half-Japanese, half-American bodyguard, to save their lives and the life of the young girl.

"Please. I'll ask you kindly one time. Step away from the girl," Ki said, still moving toward Jody.

Several of the outlaws looked at one another through hooded eyes, grinning, scowling, but frozen, it seemed, in disbelief for a critical few seconds by the ballsiness of Ki. He was almost right on top of Jody.

Jessie looked at the girl, Christine, who looked back at her, uncertain, her face red with welts, blood trickling from the side of her mouth.

"What's with this kindly shit, mister?" Jody sneered. "What, you some kinda city-slickin' sissy with that fancy talk."

"Step away from the girl."

Jody snarled, "Why you rotten . . . Ain't no man give me orders!"

9

And all hell broke loose.

Jody almost cleared leather. He would have, but his hand was disconnected from his arm in the next heartbeat. The sword had snaked from Ki's scabbard in the blink of an eye and slashed clean through Jody's wrist. The gun and the bloody piece of severed meat dropped to the ground. Jody screamed like a banshee.

The other outlaws reached for their guns. But Jessie beat them to the draw, her .38 Colt out and cracking a round that drilled through the forehead of the gunslinger closest to Jody in a sickening crack of bone. He dropped like a felled steer.

Shouts and curses mingled with the bone-chilling shrieking of Jody, as he hit the ground on his knees, clutching his stump, blood spurting away in a thick crimson stream from the useless appendage.

Jessie leapt off her mare, hit the ground with catlike grace, and tracked on with her Colt. She triggered another round, but it was a hasty shot, and it tore into the knee of one of the two mounted outlaws, who dropped his weapon and slammed to the ground, his screams adding to the din ripping from Jody's mouth.

With three running steps, Ki hit a small boulder. His *katana* winked sunlight as he vaulted off the boulder and out of the shade, blade drawn back for a lethal swipe at the mounted outlaw beside him. The outlaw swung his .44 Colt in Ki's direction, but his mount whinnied in panic and started to buck. In midair, Ki drove his sword, its edge honed to a razor sharpness, clean through the neck of that outlaw. The decapitated head sailed through the air, and the mount bolting forward, throwing its headless rider off the saddle after a few yards, blood geysering from the stump of his neck.

The outlaw Jessie had shot in the knee picked up his discarded .44 Remington and began searching for a target through the wall of dust washing over him. Jody grabbed his shotgun.

Ki raced beside a fleeing horse, hidden for a second from the view of the other outlaws as they scrambled to shoot back. Peeling off the flank of his animal shield, Ki swept over two outlaws, his blade flashing as it skewered one of the gunmen in the stomach, a bloody tip of steel jutting out the man's back for a second before Ki drew the sword back and let him topple, facedown in a pool of gore. He pivoted, ready to cut the life out of more vermin, and found the other outlaw less than six feet away from him. Then blood spurted from the hole in that outlaw's chest. Jessie at her lethal best, Ki knew, and moved on.

Screaming, Jody stumbled away from Christine, trying desperately to aim the shotgun at Jessie with one hand.

"You bastards!" Christine shouted, galvanized by hate and vengeance as she stood and snatched up the severed hand with the gun, the hand falling off the .44 Colt as she drew down on Jody.

The outlaw with the shot-out knee was fanning his .44 Remington, trying like hell to hit Ki, but Ki dropped to the ground and rolled away from bullets whining off stone behind him.

Jody's boot clipped a rock. As he began to fall, the Colt in Christine's tiny fist cracked. A split second later, Jody was screaming louder than before as the slug ripped into his groin.

Ki jumped to his feet and sent the *katana* spinning away, a silvery blur twirling through the air. As the blade thudded into the outlaw's wounded leg, two holes opened in his chest, shredding cloth, spraying blood.

Cries of horses scrambling pell-mell from the deathbed faded to whinnies.

"You bastard!"

Jessie and Ki turned grim attention on Christine as she ran up to Jody, her face livid with hate and rage.

"Ah . . . ahhhh! My nuts!" Jody wailed, clutching his ruined sac with his one good hand, his face as pale as a sheet.

Without warning, Christine tossed the Colt away and hauled up the shotgun. Jody's wide mouth was still cutting loose with screams, but Christine filled that mouth in the next moment, jamming the barrels of the shotgun into his mouth. Jody's eyes bulged with horror.

"Suck this! And he wasn't my boyfriend, he was my brother!" Christine roared, and pulled the triggers. There was a muffled double blast, and Jody's head erupted in a goreburst of flying blood, brains and bone shards. It looked as if a stick of dynamite had gone off in his mouth.

Jessie and Ki just stood their ground. Bodies twitched around them for a long moment.

The sky grew darker with the black shapes of buzzards.

Christine turned pale and wobbled, the shotgun, its barrels smoking, falling from her hands. "Oh . . . oh, God . . . How could I . . ." She stumbled back, turning her head away from the headless thing beside her. She hit her knees, and vomited.

Ki slid his sword from the leg of his victim, wiped the blood off on the man's one dry pant leg, and sheathed the *katana*. As he watched the girl, sobbing and retching, a look of pity fell over his face.

Ki looked at Jessie and said, "Play it by ear."

Jessie nodded, grim-faced.

Ki moved to the girl, who was shaking, weeping even louder. He placed his hands on her shoulders.

"It's all right," he told the girl. "You're safe now. Come on."

Tears streamed down her face as she looked up at Ki. "Where . . . What happened to Joe?"

"Your brother's dead. I'm sorry. Come on. I'll bury him."

A buzzard dipped from the swarm above, spiraling from the burning sky to feed on the dead.

Chapter 2

With a short-handled shovel he had taken off one of his victims' horses, Ki finished throwing the last bit of dirt over the body of Christine's brother. He was drenched in sweat. He flung the shovel aside, moved to his gelding, and drank from his canteen. Ki watched as Christine, silent tears rolling down her cheeks, bent over her brother's grave. She was no longer retching, no longer seemed on the verge of shock. But she was grief-stricken. Ki felt his heart ache for her; he felt her pain. She was without family, rootless, adrift all by herself in the world. He knew the feeling all too well. Something about Christine moved him, touched his soul. She seemed so innocent, yet so worldly, weak but strong. She was hard but soft. Like Jessie.

"They didn't have to kill him," she said in a small voice. "The bastards. They rode up, took our water, shot our horses right out from under us. Joe was a good man, a kind and decent man, not a mean bone in his body. They just started beatin' him, like it was fun. Went on for . . . forever it seemed. Then . . . God, then they just shot him in the stomach. Three, maybe four times. Laughed about it. So senseless, but . . . Where does it say, I suppose, that life's gotta be fair. They got theirs, that's as fair as it can get. The world will be a lot better place without them, but there's a big hole inside of me now, feel like my world's been shattered. He . . . Tomorrow was Joe's birthday." She let out a small strangled laugh. She brushed away her tears and looked at Jessie, then Ki. "Daddy's been dead for years. Mama died in her sleep just a few months ago. Suddenly, mysteriously, no rhyme or reason. We lived in Texas, had a few cattle, nothin' big, never really had no money, but we were tight as a family. Joe wanted to be a prospector, since we didn't have nothin' goin' for us back in Texas, no family left. All we had was each other, so we sold the few cattle we had and decided we'd go to California, try our luck there. Joe wasn't no cowpoke anyways. He had a dream of findin' us a better life in California, had a dream of strikin' it rich out there, maybe runnin' his own business of some type in San Francisco." She touched the rocks heaped over the grave. She found two sticks of wood and made a cross on top of the rocks. "Good-bye, Brother, rest in peace. I hope you've gone to a better world." She stood. She was a full-figured, long-legged redhead, with creamy ivory-white skin that could get fried beet red if she stayed out in the fierce sun of the desert too long. Her jeans hugged a firm, well-rounded rump; her blouse, dirty and sweat-stained, was now plastered up against the big mounds of her pillowy breasts.

Ki saw a fire in her eyes. She was tough, he knew; she was a survivor. She'd pull her world back together somehow. She was also very beautiful, he couldn't help but notice: full ripe lips, high cheekbones, green eyes. She was a whole lot of woman, Ki judged. He saw her look at Jessie first, then his way with a flash of gratitude in those green cat eyes.

"I . . . thank you," she told Jessie and Ki. "You saved my life. Probably saved me from a fate worse than death. What about them?" she said, some venom in her voice, as she jerked a nod toward the hills to the east.

"The buzzards will take care of them," Ki said, checking the sky and finding that the buzzard circle had grown smaller in the past ten minutes as most of the scavenger birds had descended to feast on the dead. "Far as I'm concerned, they're not worth burying. A shame about the horses, but we can't round them up and take them with us. Not without raising a few eyebrows . . . where we're going."

"Understand," Jessie told Christine in soft voice, "we would've taken your brother's body to Haley, given him a decent burial. But we can't afford to take a chance on attracting unneccesary attention. We don't know if the law there is honest. They would ride back here and find those other bodies. We can't be sure our version would be believed. Those bastards were part of this Brutus gang, and we could end up finding ourselves in a worse spot than just landing in jail. It was self-defense, sure, but I don't think John Brutus would really care."

"Somebody might find them anyway," Christine pointed out.

"They might," Ki said, then looked at Jessie, a

grim smile twisting the side of his mouth. "But we'll take it as it comes."

Christine nodded. "I think . . . I understand. What are you going to do with me now?"

"Why, you can ride with us," Jessie told her. "We have some business in Haley."

"The way you two handled yourselves back there, is it some killing business?"

Jessie and Ki held their ground in tight silence.

"Your silence speaks," Christine said. "None of my business. I think, well, I think there might be a coach runs through Haley. We didn't pass through there, but we asked about it at some outpost a few miles east. Old-timer told us to stay clear of Haley, said it's a bad town full of bad men, so we didn't ride through. So could be you're right about the law maybe being dishonest there. I think he said a coach runs through there. I'm not sure, though."

"You'll be safe with us," Jessie told her.

"I believe that."

"You can stay with us as long as you have to, or like," Ki said.

"I think once we get to town, all I want is a meal, a hot bath, and a bed, I'm so tired . . . I'm just so tired . . ."

By the reins, Ki led a brown gelding, a mount he'd taken from one of the outlaws, seeing as how he'd no longer be needing it, over to Christine. He helped Christine into the saddle. She looked down at Ki and smiled.

"Thank you," she said. "You put your life at risk for me back there. You just walked right up to that bastard, bold as brass. You knew what you were going to do, didn't you? You already knew you couldn't get outta there without a fight. Why? Why did you risk your life like that for me? You didn't even have a gun."

"There is no why," Ki told her. "It was just the right thing to do. And, besides, a gun doesn't make the man anyway. Neither does a sword. It's the man who's using them." He held her look for a moment; the gratitude was unmistakable in those big green eyes. Then he turned away from her penetrating stare and mounted his own horse. Damn, but he liked this girl.

Ki looked at Jessie, who showed him a knowing smile.

Jessie climbed into the saddle of her mare. "I ever tell you you're a good man, Ki?" Jessie said.

"Not in recent memory."

"Well, you are. You're one of a kind, Ki."

Didn't he know that, Ki thought, feeling a moment's pain, a fleeting moment's bitterness over his own rootlessness in the world, fully aware of his own yearning soul on fire.

The wooden sign read, "WELCOME TO HALEY—WHERE DREAMS COME TRUE."

Jessie and Ki flanked Christine as they halted their mounts at the edge of the rise and stared down into the valley, at Haley. Shouts, laughter, and female squeals, either of pleasure of pain, hard to tell which Jessie thought, shot up the rise from the wooden buildings below. Dozens of well-saddled mounts, the rifle butts of Winchesters and Henrys jutting from their scabbards, were hitched to railings in front of two-story false-front structures. A wide dirt street divided the two rows of buildings.

At the far east end of town loomed a big wooden three-story building with giant plate-glass windows looking out over the front porch. That building was painted white, with gold trim around the roof and edges glinting sunlight and the words HOTEL HALEY proclaimed in gold paint on a black board above the porch. Three buildings near the Hotel Haley were timber skeletons—no roofs, no fronts. Maybe ten wagons, half of them covered, half uncovered, but all of them laden with wooden planks, sat near the unfinished buildings. Haley was still under construction, dreams still in the dreaming stage. Jessie saw maybe two dozen men, with holstered guns tied down to their thighs, ambling about town. Up and down the boardwalks, men holding liquor bottles laughed and fondled a few roving painted ladies in garish dresses of fine silk.

Jessie studied Ki for a moment. He looked grim, concerned as ever. No doubt, Jessie knew, this was a bad town. She also hadn't been able to avoid noticing the glances Ki had been casting toward Christine during the past couple of hours' ride from the slaughterbed back northeast to Haley. And Christine had been checking Ki out, too. Jessie sensed a silent fire building between these two. Christine, she figured, saw Ki as something of a hero, and, for damn sure, he was.

Christine read off the sign, "Where dreams come true. What kind of dreams?"

"Probably more like nightmares," Jessie said, "if the rest of these folks are anything like what we left behind for the buzzards."

"Oughta change the name of this town to Helltown," Ki said. Then without warning, as he urged his mount ahead, his foot flew out of his stirrup and smashed through the Welcome to Haley sign. Wood splinters exploded through the air, as if a bolt of lightning had shattered the sign. Ki looked back over his shoulder at Jessie's questioning face. "Have to start someplace, Jessie."

Christine looked at Ki's backside, a small smile dancing over her lips. "Take it, Ki, you don't think much of this town."

"Never have been much of a dreamer," he said over his shoulder.

"How about a romantic?" Christine asked. Jessie smiled as she caught the not-so-subtle implications of that question.

A half smile flickered over Ki's lips. "Well, now, I've been known to be that."

Jessie glimpsed the moment's spark in Christine's eyes, smiled to herself again, then gently urged her mount ahead.

Down the incline and into town the threesome slowly rode their mounts. Jessie felt eyes boring into her as they passed a livery stable, the sheriff's office, buildings with signs that said, "ROOMS." No telegraph lines, no newspaper office, but Jessie figured this town was built purposely to be cut off from the rest of the world. She felt the tension in the air, and Christine became visibly uncomfortable in the saddle as a few whistles and catcalls shot their way. Jessie noticed several curtains pulled back in the windows of boarding places. Shadows stared down at them from behind those windows.

"What . . . what are we going to do?" Christine asked. "I don't like this place. It . . . it's got a . . . wicked feel about it."

And, indeed, Jessie thought, Christine was right. The town had a mean feel to it, had an ugliness in the air about it that felt almost tangible to Jessie. She felt a creeping sensation walk down her spine, a warning that they were being watched by everybody in Haley.

"We don't like it already either," Ki said. "That's why we came. We'll get you that meal and room so you can rest."

"What are you two going to do?"

Jessie flashed a grim smile, as she raked a hard stare over the gunmen and their ladies lounging on the boardwalks. She said, "See what kind of town Haley built, see for ourselves just what kind of dreams the man had in mind. Ki," she said, jerking a nod at a place with batwings, the town saloon, most likely, she figured. Then she saw a sign over the place that read, "HALEY'S COMET— GAMES, WOMEN, ROOMS." "There's your room, Christine."

"There? That's a brothel," Christine protested.

"Like Ki said," Jessie told her, "we have to start someplace. You'll be all right. Besides, I bet this whole town is one big brothel. One place is as safe— maybe—as another."

Christine looked uncertain as they guided their mounts toward Haley's Comet. Maybe ten gunhands were lounging along the planks in front of the plate-glass window of Haley's Comet. As Jessie, Ki, and Christine dismounted and hitched their horses to the railing in front of a trough, Jessie heard more soft whistles and felt the tension build like a crackling electricity in the air.

"My, my, catch an eyeful of this, will ya, Jeb?"

"Yeah, Ollie, I'm lookin', and I damn sure like what I'm seein'."

Jessie glanced at the two gunmen licking their bristled chops. Jeb was a skinny, ferret-faced, beady-eyed gunhand, who took the cheroot out of his mouth as if he could get a better look at Jessie and Christine without the smoke in his eyes. Ollie was a short, stocky guy with an ivory-handled .44 Remington holstered for a cross draw. That was, Jessie thought, if he could reach across his whale belly to get hold of the grips.

"Jesus, you boys see any woman, you figger she's fair game. You make me sick," a chubby blond whore in a red silk dress said, her face hard as she stared at Jessie and Christine with unconcealed jealousy.

"You ain't gittin a little green on us, are ya, Candy?" a tall gunhand with a badly pockmarked face and a greasy black beard gruffed. "Whatsa matter, 'fraid they might cut into some a yer payin' paper," he said with a laugh, then sucked from a bottle of whiskey.

"Fat chance, Crawford," Candy growled back.

Crawford laughed again. "Everytime I git in bed wich ya, Candy, that's what I'm takin'. A fat chance!"

The gunhands roared with laughter.

Then they looked at Ki with suspicion and hostility. A hard silence fell over the planks in front of Haley's Comet as Jessie, Ki, and Christine stepped up onto the boardwalk. Mean-eyed stares looked Ki up and down, gazes lingering over his sword for long moments.

A bowlegged gunman, his cheek bulging out from a wad of tobacco, squished a thick, gummy stream

23

of brown juice out into the street, his hand draped over the butt of a Colt Frontier double-action .45. "Hell's this boy s'pposed to be? Sure 'nuff hearda gunfighters, fellers. Never seen a swordfighter out this way."

Ki ignored the remark.

Jeb stepped up to Jessie, blocking her path. He smiled, baring a set of crooked, tobacco-stained teeth. "Hey, sweetness, you here lookin' fer work? Jist step inside, go see the Preacher and the big bald one, name a Pluto. Preacher-turned-pimp, how 'bout that? You can whore and have yer soul saved at the same time."

Jessie felt her head wanting to spin with nausea from the stench blasting out of Jeb's mouth. She held her ground for a tight moment, then showed Jeb a cold smile. "No, thanks," she said. "Sorry to disappoint you," she said, then brushed past the gunman, headed for the batwings.

As the sounds of laughter, clinking glasses, and clattering chips assaulted her ears, Jessie stopped and heard Jeb snarl at Ki, "Hell are you s'pposed to be, boy? Fancy sword, long hair like some Injun. Got slanty-type eyes on ya, though. You some kinda half-breed?"

Jessie saw Ki tense, saw the familiar rage in his eyes. Then Ki just smiled. A street fight was beneath him, she knew.

"I could be your worst nightmare, if you don't get out of my way," Ki told Jeb in a quiet voice edged with steel.

"I don't like the looks of you." Jeb pushed on. "Come ridin' in here with two sweet-lookin' pieces a tail, like yer some kinda stud. Don't look like all

24

that much to me. You watch your step. Got me?"

"Oh, I got you, all right," Ki said, then took Christine by the arm and stepped up behind Jessie.

As Jessie, Ki, and Christine pushed through the batwings, Jessie heard one of the gunhands behind her say, "Wonder where the hell Jody and Jimbo are? S'pposed to been here by now. Big John's got business he needs those boys to take care of with 'im."

"Fuck 'em," someone else rasped. "It'll git taken care of. They git here when they git here. Jist grab hold of some of Candy and ride her like a buckin' bronco."

"Can't miss there. Whole lot to grab holda!"

There was another outburst of laughter.

"Screw you!" Candy snarled.

"No, I'll screw you!"

Jessie cast Ki a hard, knowing look.

"Maybe we should've buried them after all," Ki whispered, standing right beside Jessie.

Once again, Jessie felt all eyes drilling into them. The gaming-whoring saloon was packed with customers and whores. It was a big place inside. There were maybe a dozen large round felt-covered tables on one side of the room—poker games, faro, and keno. Cigar smoke hung over the heads of the players. Chips were flying; whiskey and beer was being sucked down like there was no tomorrow; keno goose pellets were clattering, and card cutters were snipping off the edges of cards with scissors, to extend the life of those cards. Blondes, brunettes, and redheads in a wild array of silk and lace hovered around the players, their eyes hungry for more than just some gambling action. A long mahogany bar ran the length of the room, opposite the gaming action.

Two bartenders in white aprons were in almost constant motion, swiftly moving back and forth from three tiers of liquor bottles, waiting on the long line of bearded, grim-faced gunhands at the bar.

Jessie, Ki, and Christine found a space at the bar. They sat on their stools, Christine between Jessie and Ki.

"What can I get you?" a bartender gruffed at them.

"Coffee," Jessie said.

"Same here," Ki told him. "How about a steak for the lady here," he said, nodding at Christine.

The bartender grumbled, "Comin' up," then moved off.

Jessie and Ki checked out the players. In the far corner, at the foot of the steps, Jessie saw a man in a loud red-and-white pin-striped suit, so tight it threatened to bust at the seams, sitting at a table, a cigar in his mouth. He had a sharp face, with greedy eyes that watched the room through drifting smoke. He was short and pudgy, but there was a mean look about him, Jessie decided. He had dark eyes that glittered like the skin of a diamondback. And the giant who sat beside Pinstripes looked twice as mean. He wore a black suit, a black derby, and had black eyes, like two bits of coal, his skin as pale as a sheet. Pluto, she assumed. The pimp and his muscle.

"How ya doin', folks?"

Jessie, Ki, and Christine turned just as the bartender set down two cups of steaming coffee in front of them.

"I'm Madame Cheri."

Madame Cheri wore a flaming red silk dress with lace around the edges. She was a big woman, close to six feet tall, and fat, too, her girdle snug around her big belly, folds of fat threatening to pop open her dress. She reeked of perfume, and her face was so painted with makeup she looked ghoulish to Jessie.

"Never seen you around here before," she said, her voice deep but raspy from whiskey and smokes. She popped a cheroot in her mouth and scratched a match off the barfront. She took several deep puffs, her eyes narrowing as she studied Jessie and Christine. "You two lookin' for work maybe?" she asked.

Just then, Jessie saw Jeb and four of his cronies push through the batwings. They were looking Jessie and Christine over with unconcealed lust. She saw Jeb say something to the beefy one, Ollie, and both gunmen then sneered at Ki's back. They stood there, unmoving, watching the three at the bar as buzzards would a dying animal.

"We're just passing through," Jessie said, feeling her blood race with anger. Next time someone asked her if she wanted work whoring . . . well, she wasn't sure what she'd do, she just knew it wouldn't be good. "All we want's a meal, and a place to sleep for the night. Just want to be left alone."

Madame Cheri blew smoke over Jessie's head. "All three of ya want a room together? Single bed, I bet. Tight little threesome, how cozy."

"No. It's not like that at all," Jessie said. "But I could see how *you* might think like that."

Madame Cheri shrugged and blew smoke again, but this time at the back of Jessie's head. "No need to get snooty, honey. You change yer mind about work, that's the man to see over there," she said, nodding over her shoulder. "That's *the man*, in the pinstripes. Mr. Edwards."

Jessie snorted.

Madame Cheri scowled. "What's the noise about, missy? You too good to do it for money or somethin'?"

"Or something," Jessie said, trying to control her anger.

"How 'bout you?" Madame Cheri said, moving up behind Ki. "Don't look like these two fancy ladies give it up so easy. Got plenty of girls just be itchin' to climb in the saddle with a good-lookin' hunk of man like yourself."

Jessie saw Ki clench his jaw. He sipped his coffee, ignoring Madame Cheri.

"I'm talkin' to you, mister. Maybe you don't speak English."

"Speak English just fine," Ki said.

"All right, now we're gettin' somewhere. Let me put it to ya in plain English then. You wanna screw?"

Ki cracked a wry grin. "You?"

The madam scowled and then looked puzzled for a moment. "No . . . no, one of my girls."

"Do I have to pay for it?"

Now Madame Cheri's scowl turned menacing. "What are you, some kind of smart ass? Of course, you have to pay."

"No, thanks." Ki sniffed, still grinning. "I've got a little higher standards than that."

"Why, you shit!"

"Problem here, Madame?"

Jessie turned. Jeb and his boys had crept up right behind Ki's back.

"Yeah, these folks think they're too damn good for us," Madame Cheri growled. "They got problems awright, attitude problems. This one here," she said, jabbing a fat finger at Ki, "he just insulted me and my girls. Thinks he's too good to pay for it."

"Is that so?" Jeb said. "Now I told you, boy, to watch yerself. You didn't listen. Now . . . well, now, I think I'm gonna have to teach you some respect."

Ki sighed, looking irritated, staring into his coffee cup.

"What's the problem over there?"

The room fell silent.

Jessie saw Pluto rise from his seat, a dark scowl on his face.

"Nothin' I can't handle, Pluto," Jeb called across the room. "These strangers don't like yer hospitality, just insulted yer Madame and yer girls."

Pluto chuckled, a deep throaty rumble that blasted through the thick silence. "So, take care of it. Man to man. I'll even put down fifty on you, Jeb. You lose, though, you'll answer to me."

"I'll throw down twenty on Jeb," someone called out from the crowd. "Ain't had a good fight in a while. Not one we can all bet on anyways."

"The stranger ain't got no gun," someone else said.

"Hand to hand then," Pluto said. "Is that a problem for you, Jeb?"

Jeb seemed uncertain, but he'd put himself in no position to back out, not with the house backing him. He licked his lips, nervous. Voices, cut with laughter, called out their bets. No one was betting on Ki, Jessie noticed.

"Off with the sword," Jeb told Ki.

Jessie held Ki's stare. There was no way out. They'd been looking to play it low-key, but now they were about to make some noise.

"I don't fight for money," Ki said.

"You're gonna fight, or you're gonna die right here," Ollie chimed in.

"Okay. Since you insist. Step back," Ki told Jeb, after a long, tight moment of silence.

Jeb moved back. He unbuckled his gunbelt and handed it to Ollie. "Now you."

Ki removed his scabbard and laid it down on the bar top.

Ollie stepped up next to the sword and said, "I'll watch this."

Ki bored a threatening look into Ollie's eyes as he backed away from the bar. "I'll kindly ask you one time, do not touch it."

Ollie seemed set to curse, but said nothing.

With slow, measured steps, Ki moved out into an area clear of tables. A hard silence held everyone in the room in a tight grip of fear and anticipation.

Jeb grinned at Ki. "Kiley," he said over his shoulder, holding out his hand.

Jessie saw the bowlegged gunman step up to Jeb. She was sure Kiley was going to hand Jeb a gun, but a large Bowie knife came whipping out from behind Kiley's back. Jessie looked at Ki, who shook his head and chuckled.

Jeb took the knife and advanced on Ki. "I'm gonna gut you, boy, strangle ya with yer own yella guts. Think you'll be snickerin' then?"

"What the hell gives here!?"

A big broad-shouldered man burst through the batwings. Jessie saw the star pinned to his chest.

"Jist in time, Sheriff Doughty," Ollie called across the room, "to place yer bet, that is."

Sheriff Doughty took his hand away from his Colt

Peacemaker, his clean-shaven, sun-burnished features set in a hard expression as he looked from Jeb to Ki. He grunted, moving toward the gaming tables.

"Well," the sheriff said, "I see Jeb there with a blade, the stranger with empty hands. Don't seem like much of a fair fight. I got ten bucks on Jeb."

"Hey," someone called out. "Seems to me, with no one betting on Long Hair, hell, he ain't put up nothin'."

"He just did."

All eyes turned to the preacher-turned-pimp. Edwards took the cigar out of his mouth, his eyes glinting with laughter. "He just put up his two lady friends. He loses, everybody here gets a turn at those two. On the house."

Low laughter rumbled through the room.

Jessie felt cold fear clutch at her heart.

Chapter 3

They looked like a pack of hungry wolves to Jessie.

All but one man.

She hadn't seen him when they'd first walked into Haley's Comet, but now she couldn't help but notice him. The stranger sat at the end of the bar, alone. He was the only one in the room who hadn't called in a bet, the wager being Ki's hide for her and Christine's flesh. He was dressed in black, from Stetson to long coat and vest and Levis, down to his scuffed, spurless boots. The clothes looked too small on him to Jessie; she noticed that he had unusually wide shoulders and well-defined arm and thigh muscles that bulged against the seams. His big, long-fingered, weathered hands rested on the bar top near his glass of beer, and he wore a holstered .44 Remington tied-down by a leather thong to his thigh. He had short black hair, and his face was clean-shaven, with a square jaw, high cheekbones, a sharp, narrow nose, and flared nostrils. He had the bluest eyes she'd ever seen.

The man looked as mean as anybody in there, but there was something behind his eyes, a hint of compassion maybe, Jessie thought. He seemed to pretend he wasn't the least bit interested in the fight to the death about to take place behind him, but she saw him glance her way. And there was a flash of something in his penetrating gaze, something that told her she, Christine, and Ki weren't alone. Jessie felt her breath catch in her throat for a second. The stranger was one of the most handsome dark-haired men she'd ever laid eyes on.

But she turned grim attention to the fight about to get under way behind her. She didn't doubt the outcome, but if the pack decided they didn't want to play fair, she would go down fighting; she wasn't about to be sport for a cutthroat lawless mob itching to gang rape her and Christine.

The outcome quickly became apparent, as Jeb bulled in, slashing at Ki's face with his Bowie knife.

It ended even quicker, and in the most painful and horrible way for Jeb.

Jeb missed, and Ki stepped back. Jeb drove the blade back, but the edge of the knife only swiped at air, Ki ducking under it, quick as a cat. Then Ki made his move, attacking as fast as a wink of lightning. Jeb started to thrust the knife at Ki's face, but Ki's hand shot out and grabbed Jeb's wrist in a viselike grip. Ki speared a knee into the other man's gut, and a belch of air blasted from Jeb's mouth as he doubled over. Ki then chopped an elbow over the back of Jeb's head and lowered himself to explode upward like an erupting volcano and, with the heel of his free hand, smash Jeb's nose. There was a sickening squelch of bone and blood spraying from the pulped ruins of Jeb's sniffer. He yelled in agony, but Ki wasn't finished. The knife clattered to the floor, Ki still holding Jeb's arm out by the wrist. Ki wrenched the arm up and around, looking down at Jeb's elbow with savage determination in his dark, narrowed gaze. Jeb screamed through his bloody mask. The only other sound in the room was the lone gasp of a whore.

Out of the corner of her eye, Jessie saw a big man with straight shoulder-length brown hair step out of a side room behind the stairs that were off to the side of the gaming tables. He had a handlebar mustache, a beaked nose like a hawk, and dark, piercing eyes. Right away, Jessie recognized him from Wanted posters at Starbuck outposts. John Brutus. The big outlaw just stood behind the players, watching the action with an indifferent expression.

Ki twisted Jeb's arm upward, forcing him to his knees. As Jeb hit his knees, Ki raised his free arm, his eyes blazing with fury. He sounded a chilling bellow, an ear-piercing *kiai*, spirit yell, then drove his elbow down through Jeb's forearm, just below his victim's elbow. A shriek of agony instantly ripped from Jeb's mouth as Ki splintered the man's arm with a loud crack of bone that sounded like a twig snapping in half. Bloody, jagged bone shards tore through the cloth of Jeb's shirt. It was a new but very effective version, Jessie thought, of the *hizi-otoshi*, elbow drop.

"Jesus!" Madame Cheri gasped.

Ki released Jeb, who kept screaming. As tears poured down Jeb's cheeks, Ki stepped back, then hammered a snapkick square into Jeb's mouth. Jeb hit the floor on his back. Semi-conscious, he began spitting blood and teeth out of his mouth, gagging and whimpering.

"Why, you dirty bastard!" Ollie snarled, drawing his .45.

Jessie was reaching for her gun, but the blue-eyed stranger had already bolted off his seat, anticipating the ambush. He was so quick, Jessie froze, amazed at his speed and daring. The Remington was out of his holster as fast as a rattler would strike from the brush, the hammer cocked and the muzzle jammed against the base of Ollie's skull in the next heartbeat.

"Fair's fair," the stranger said. "The man won. Let it be, if you know what's good for you."

"Hey, c'mon, stranger," Sheriff Doughty called out, trying to inject some bluster into his quivering voice. "No need for that. It's over, like you said. The man won."

For a moment, Jessie expected someone else in the room to draw down. The preacher-pimp and his muscle looked disappointed Jeb hadn't won their bet. As did every other man in the room. Except the stranger in black.

"You want to collect your money?" the stranger said to Ki.

Ki didn't move, just held the stranger's gaze, the storm still raging in his eyes. Silently, Ki, Jessie knew, was telling the stranger, and everyone else there, he'd collect his bet when he was damn good and ready. And he could, Jessie thought, sensing the fear and newfound respect of every man in that place for her bodyguard.

Jeb was now vomiting, blubbering like a baby.

"Put it back, Ollie. Now."

Heads turned and eyes fell on John Brutus. His presence commanded everyone's attention.

"Shit," Ollie rasped through clenched teeth. "This ain't over," he hissed at Ki.

"It better be," the stranger said in an icy voice.

Ollie dropped his Colt back in its holster.

"Everybody pay the man," John Brutus called out in a voice that rolled over the room like a peal of thunder. "Ollie, get that sack of shit off the floor and out of here."

And then John Brutus wheeled and vanished back into the side room from where he'd first appeared.

Ollie lumbered over to Jeb. "Come on, you heard John."

Whimpering and cursing Ki, Jeb stood, his shattered arm hanging, limp and bloody, by his side, vomit and blood running down his shirt. "You bastard, I'll git you for this, I'll kill you, you broke my fuckin' arm!" he cried through his shattered mouth. "I'll git you!"

"C'mon!" Ollie urged, and led Jeb out through the batwings.

Jessie looked at the stranger, as he uncocked and holstered his weapon. He wasn't tall, maybe six feet, but he was muscular, solid as a rock, and looked as strong as a horse.

Jessie showed the stranger a grateful smile. "Thank you, Mr. . . ."

"Stone, Joe Stone."

"I'm Jessie. This is Christine. And thanks again. That was real decent of you. It wasn't your fight."

Stone said nothing, just nodded.

"Yeah, I reckon I owe you some thanks, too, Mr.

Stone," Christine said. "Nice to see there's at least one gentleman in this town. Besides Ki, that is."

Stone cocked an appreciative grin at Christine. "Ki. Your friend who snapped that guy's arm like a stick?"

Jessie nodded, a trace of pride in her smile. "That's Ki."

"You seem like real fine ladies. Looks like your man, Ki, can take care of the both of you, but be careful just the same."

"You don't strike me as the gambling type, Mr. Stone," Jessie said, as she saw Ki moving through the crowd, rounding up his cash, some of the players scowling and grumbling, but parting with their money anyway.

"No."

"You're not like this other vermin that infests this town. Makes me wonder maybe what you might be doing here," Jessie said.

"I could wonder the same thing about you."

Jessie held Stone's gaze for a second. There was something about him, his commanding presence, the aura of strength and confidence, the sense of decency and fair play, and once again, she felt her breath wanting to lock up in her throat. He was also a mystery, and Jessie liked her men with a touch of mystery to them.

"Would you mind if I got my beer and joined you ladies?" Stone asked. "I could use a little friendly company. As you can see it's a little tough making friends in this town, and the kind of friendly they provide here, well, it's not my idea of friendly."

It didn't seem like a come-on to Jessie, at least not on the surface. She was about to tell Stone he could join them when Sheriff Doughty rolled up behind them.

"Suggest you people walk real careful in my town from here on."

"And some town it is, Sheriff," Stone said, steel in his voice. "Where even the sheriff places a bet on a man's life. You sure it's your town?"

Sheriff Doughty looked flustered, his face flushing with embarrassment and anger. "Don't know what your business is here, mister, nor you, missy," he said to Jessie. "But I'll warn you again, walk real careful, real light, like you're walkin' on broken glass and don't wanna get cut. Get out of line, I'll wing you behind bars so fast you won't know what hit you."

Doughty spun on his heels and headed for the batwings.

The stranger went to get his beer from the end of the bar. Jessie watched his backside. Who was he? What was he doing in Haley? The way he talked to the sheriff, all but telling him he and his town were as dirty as horse manure, the way he carried himself, the cold, scrutinizing business look in his steely eyes—there was a whole lot more to Joe Stone, Jessie sensed, than he was letting on.

"Jessie," Christine said, "if you don't mind, I'd like to get that room now. I just . . . I just don't want to sit here in this . . . place. I don't mean any offense, I don't mean like it's not all right if you do."

"No offense taken. I understand," Jessie said. "You need some rest anyway." She said that with a straight face, but she knew Christine had Ki on her mind. She wondered how Christine was going to go about

39

getting what she really wanted.

Ki returned to the bar. He took half of the wad of cash and handed Jessie the other half. Then he picked up his sword and slid the scabbard inside his sash.

"What's this for?" Jessie asked. "You earned it, not me."

"Yeah," Ki said, smiling, "but you provided the motivation. You didn't think I was about to lose you, the both of you, to, as Christine here said earlier, a fate worse than death."

Joe Stone returned. He looked at Ki and said, "Don't mind if I join you and the ladies, do you?"

"Not at all," Ki answered. "Thanks for what you did."

"You handled yourself real well," Stone said. "But, you never know, you might need someone to watch your back again. That is, if you plan on hanging around Haley."

There was a moment's silence, as Jessie saw that Ki didn't know what to make of Stone's remark.

"Listen, uh, Ki," Christine said, "I told Jessie, I'm awful tired. I was wondering if maybe you wouldn't mind helping me get a room, and walking me there."

Jessie turned away from Ki and Christine, feeling the trace of a smile tug at her lips. "Go ahead, Ki, I'll be fine here with Mr. Stone."

"I mean, I wouldn't mind spending the night here, good a place as any in this town," Christine went on, "long as I know you—and Jessie—are close by. I'll worry about what I'm gonna do tomorrow."

Out of the corner of her eye, Jessie saw Ki hold Christine's stare. The fire was building. And she didn't think it would be long before those flames were crackling loud, real loud. Christine was trying to play it smooth as silk, and coy, but she was obvious. Ki didn't seem to mind.

"What about that steak?" Ki asked her.

"Maybe you could bring it up to me later."

Ki held his arm out in the direction of the pimp and his muscle. "Looks like the only way upstairs is past them. Come on, I'll see you up. The room's on me."

As Ki led Christine away from the bar, Jessie smiled into her coffee cup. Something told her it was going to be a while before she saw Ki and Christine again.

Then Joe Stone sat beside her. And she felt her own fire building. He was a whole lot of man; this stranger in black named Stone was having an effect on her, quickly, too quickly she thought, but she couldn't help herself. There was also something deadly serious about Joe Stone. He was in Haley for a reason, and she wanted to know what his business there was, hoping it didn't interfere with her vendetta. Gut instinct, however, was telling her they could be on a collision course.

She didn't like to use her feminine wiles, seduction, as a way to pry information out of a man, but, she thought, and tried to suppress a grin, if she could kill two birds with one stone, it might prove to be a whole lot of fun. Besides, she knew Stone was right. She and Ki did plan on hanging around Haley until they found a way to get to Max Haley and crush his dreams. And they just might need someone to watch their backs, after all.

● ● ●

Something told Ki, too, that it was going to be a while before he saw Jessie again. But that's the way he wanted it. The way Christine was looking at him, trying to hide her hunger with ladylike dignity but coming up short with those little sly glances she cast toward him, told him he could be finding a room for the night, too. The same room as Christine.

Leading Christine by the arm, he pulled up in front of the pimp's table. Edwards stared at him through his cigar smoke, and Pluto glared at Ki, then looked Christine up and down.

"How much for a room?" Ki asked.

The pimp chuckled. "You didn't like my Madame's offer to put your girls to work for me, huh? I don't take rejection lightly."

"I'm not any whore, mister," Christine snapped.

"Sure, you're not," the pimp said, leaning back in his chair. "I'm gonna tell you this, because I'm a fair and honest man," he said, staring at Christine. "Somehow, some way, I'm going to own you. You'll be working for me. Someone that looks like you, you can make me, and yourself, a whole lot of money."

Christine bared her teeth. "Why, you bastard . . ."

Ki had the urge to smash the pimp's nose in with a backhand hammer-fist. He grabbed Christine by the arm before she could take a swing at Edwards. She backed off.

"She wants a room for the night. Single bed," Ki told the pimp. "And I'll tell you something. It'll be over my dead body before she or my other lady friend whore for you."

"And what are you, her keeper?" Pluto asked.

"You gonna stand outside her door all night and protect her?"

"You some kind of guardian angel for the little lass?" The preacher-turned-pimp chuckled.

"If I have to be. The room. How much?"

"For you," Edwards said, an oily smile spreading over his weasel face, "twenty bucks."

"I could buy a whole floor for that," Ki said.

Edwards blew smoke in Ki's face. "Take it or leave it. I got clout in this town, stranger. I spread a bad word about you, you won't find a room under fifty. You'll be sleeping out in the cold tonight."

Ki flipped the cash down in front of Edwards, the whole amount of the unarmed robbery.

Edwards slid a key across the table. "Room five."

Christine picked up the key.

After raking a cold eye over Edwards and Pluto, Ki followed Christine up the stairs, several whores passing them on their way down into the gaming room and casting Ki approving looks.

"Hey, handsome," one whore crooned.

"Nice ass," another purred.

"Bet you got a big stick for a lady to ride," a blonde said.

"Ki," Christine said, moving down the long, narrow hall, obviously relieved to be away from the whores and their crude remarks, "I'm not really like this . . . I mean I don't mean to sound forward . . . but . . ." She stopped at room five, put the key in the door, and unlocked it. "But would you stay with me for a while? I'm scared, I'm still shakin' all over . . . This whole day has been a nightmare. I don't want to be alone right now."

Ki nodded and looked deep into her eyes. He

43

showed her a warm smile and felt a fire stir in his loins. Yes, he believed her, she wasn't like *that*, meaning she wasn't a whore. And she was scared, she did feel all alone, her brother, her only family, now gone. His heart ached for her. Just as it had back on the desert when he'd buried her brother. He saw her looking at him funny then, with a sort of hero worship in her eyes. He felt as strong, as proud, as he ever had; his pride always swelled some when women looked up to him with want and admiration. He was glad he'd been there for her, had saved her life. He only wished he could have saved her brother's life, too.

He followed her into the small, spartanly furnished room. There was a single brass bed and a stand with a kerosene lamp beside the bed. Christine closed the door behind her. Ki moved toward the window and stared out at the barren brown hills to the north. He felt his heart grow heavy for some reason, the stink of death still in his nose, the memories of the day's violence locking him up inside himself. He was worried about Jessie, too. This was one of the worst towns they had ever ridden into. And just who the hell was this Stone? What was his game?

"Ki."

Her voice, hitting his back, soft and yearning.

Ki turned as Christine moved toward him with slow, uncertain steps. He saw the fire in her eyes.

"Ki, I've . . . I don't know what it is about you, I mean, I've only known you for a few hours . . . but it's like, I don't know, it's like I've known you all my life . . . or have been looking for a man like you. Strong, brave. And handsome. Don't make me ask . . . Don't make me beg," she said, unbuttoning her

44

blouse. "I've only ever done it once before, that was more than a year ago. He was one of my brother's friends. I just feel like . . . like I've got to have you . . . or I'll die . . ."

"Sssshhh," Ki said, laying a gentle finger on her full, ripe lips. He felt her tongue dart lightly out of her mouth and touch the tip of his finger, her eyes burning with desire. "Say no more." He slipped her blouse off and stared down at the milky white mounds of her breasts, feeling himself swelling already, his manhood straining against the crotch of his pants. Her breasts were large and firm, and he cupped one then the other. She moaned, her eyes fluttering shut.

He kissed her on the mouth. She seemed to breathe a fiery wind down his throat as she greedily locked on his mouth and darted her tongue past his lips. He felt strong, in control, big and powerful, and he wanted her bad, too. Suddenly, without warning, she put her hand on his bulge, massaging it.

"Oh, God . . . Oh, God . . . ," she said, pulling back, staring down at him in awe and hunger.

They undressed, quickly, and Ki saw her shuddering with anticipation, her musk filling his nose as she stretched out on the bed. Ki's member wobbled some, jutting up near his belly, as he walked toward her.

"Oh, God! It's so big. It's so beautiful!" she gasped, eyes wide, as she kneeled on the edge of the bed. She took him in her mouth.

Ki stood, feeling waves of pleasure roll down his spine as her hot, slippery mouth stroked him, licked him, up and down. She cupped his sac, gently squeezing it, as she tried to take the length of his pole all the way into her mouth, but couldn't. Drool ran from her wet mouth, slicking him. With her hand, she stroked him with a fury, moaning. Her mouth was so wet, so hot, her hand so strong as she tried to milk him off, Ki felt himself on the verge of exploding, but he held back. He pulled her off him and laid her down. She opened her legs, pulling her knees back. She moaned, "Be gentle, please . . ." She wanted gentle, but she was like a she-demon, a wildcat, her eyes blazing with desire as she stared up at Ki. "Oh, I knew it, I knew you were all man . . ."

Ki mounted her and kissed her fiery lips. Slowly, he entered her, sliding gently, deep into her sopping and very tight cavern. She writhed and bucked, grinding herself into his loins, thrashing and moaning, clawing her fingers into the corded muscles of his back.

"Oh . . . oh!" she cried.

Ki found his rhythm, but she was already tightening around him as she built toward orgasm. He pulled out and she cried out, "No!"

He lay down beside her and locked his lips on one of her breasts, her nipple hard as a thimble as he sucked it. She spread her legs and rolled over on top of him. She took his shaft in her hands and guided him into her, whimpering, shuddering, as she eased down onto the whole length of him. He kneaded her firm cheeks, spreading her ass wide. Her cries became growling sounds as she rubbed her hardened button, up and down, against his pole. She dug her fingers into his chest, her body wracked by one long convulsion that seemed to go on forever as she cried, "I'm . . . I'm . . ."

She came.

She let out a gasp of contentment, sweat forming a sheen on her face. "What . . . what about you?"

Ki eased her off him, guided her onto her hands and knees, and entered her from behind. She gasped again, writhing, bucking back against him. He spread her cheeks wide. Her flesh was so soft, so creamy, he seemed to grow harder just by the very sight, the very feel, of her ass.

"I'm . . . I'm . . ." she cried, and shuddered with another orgasm.

Ki felt himself about to erupt as he speared her harder and harder. Then he exploded and felt himself drenching her, cooling the fire deep in her belly. She reached around, grabbing him by the back of his head, tugging at his hair, moaning, "Oh . . . oh, I feel it . . . so deep . . ."

Ki kissed her shoulders, spent. Even after his orgasm, he stayed hard for a full minute, just left himself inside her sopping tunnel, let her feel it, let her want it some more. Finally he felt himself begin to shrink and slipped out of her.

"Stay with me for a while?" she purred, lying down on her back, mussing up Ki's hair. "You'll stay, won't you?"

"I'll stay."

He kissed her, her breath filling his mouth.

Stone had sat in silence since Ki left with Christine. Jessie sensed he had something on his mind that he was wrestling with telling her. There was no one sitting on either side of them. The games had gotten back into full swing; it was as if the fight had never happened. Beer flowed, men laughed, and whores whored.

Stone's expression turned ever more serious. He leaned close to Jessie. "Jessie. I trust you. I'm pretty good at reading people. I have a feeling you aren't just passing through."

Jessie stared into Stone's blue eyes. "You have something you want to say, feel free."

Stone leaned a little closer, checking behind him to make sure no one was listening. He lowered his voice to a near whisper. "I'm a bounty hunter. I'm here to clean up this town."

Jessie felt her heart skip a beat. Collision course.

"Well, you were right, Mr. Stone. I'm not passing through either. I think we'd better talk."

"Let's get out of here. I have a room across the street, if that's all right. We can talk in private there."

Jessie nodded. There was a lot she wanted to talk to Stone about, too.

Chapter 4

Stone handed Jessie a dozen Wanted posters. They were in Stone's room, a small second-story sweatbox overlooking the street, directly across from Haley's Comet. Seated on the lone wooden chair in that room, beside the brass bed, Jessie scoured the posters. A dozen outlaw faces stared back at her, all of them wanted, DEAD OR ALIVE. Of the dozen outlaws, John Brutus had the biggest bounty on his head, ten thousand dollars, with a two-thousand-dollar bonus for bringing him in just plain dead.

"There's more scum here than those twelve you see with money on their hides," Stone told Jessie, scratching a match off the lamp stand and firing up a cheroot as a lone fly buzzed around the room. "At least another dozen I've seen already in this town, wanted by federal marshals. Rape, robbery, murder, cattle rustling."

"Looks like you could stand to make a small fortune," Jessie said, handing the Wanted posters back

49

to Stone, who folded them and tucked them inside his jacket. "That is, if you live to collect."

Stone looked out the window, hard-eyed. "Oh, I'll collect. Or I'll die trying."

"What about Max Haley? Does he fit into your plans?"

Stone looked at Jessie, smoke curling out his flared nostrils. "You ask that like you've got something in mind for Haley. Sounds personal."

"It is, and I do. That's the reason we're talking in private. Something told me when I first saw you that you were here for business, same kind of business Ki and I are here for—killing business. I wanted us to have this talk so we could reach an understanding, so we're not tripping over each other's feet, or getting caught in the each other's cross fire. What I'm saying is you can have Brutus and whoever else you want; you can have anybody but Max Haley."

"What's so special about Haley?"

"I'll be up front with you, Mr. Stone."

"Joe."

Jessie looked Joe dead in the eye. A half smile danced over her lips. She sensed that they could reach that understanding. "Okay. Joe. Haley is part of an organization that murdered my father a long time ago."

A grim smile cut Stone's mouth as he lipped his cheroot. Then the smile vanished as a haunted looked filled his eyes. "Vengeance. I can understand that. Okay, you can have Haley. There's no price on his head."

"You make it sound like I should thank you for being so gracious."

"Thank me when we ride out of here. Alive and in one piece. And with a wagon full of dead outlaws."

Stone fell silent, and Jessie studied him. She thought she saw pain flicker through his eyes, the pain of bitter memories, as he stared out the window. She felt compelled to know more about this man.

"There's more to this," she said, "than just a purely mercenary angle, isn't there?"

"Yeah. There is. You're a very perceptive lady . . . just like . . ." Stone's voice trailed off as he sucked on his cheroot and blew out a long, thin line of blue-gray smoke. Slowly, he moved to the bed and sat. "I was a lawman, years ago. Colorado. I lost my badge. One too many notches on my belt, you might say. I wasn't trigger-happy; things just happened. I never killed a man who didn't draw down on me first. I drifted for a while after they took my badge, did some logging in the northwest, rode with a cattle company in northern Colorado for a spell. Then I met a woman." A distant look filled Stone's eyes.

"She was the most beautiful woman I'd ever seen." He cast a glance at Jessie. "She had strawberry blond hair, like yours, the greenest eyes you'd ever seen, too. She was a good woman, had a heart as big as the sky. She was the kindest person, man or woman, I'd ever met, full of life, cared about me like I never dreamed any woman ever could. Well, I built us a cabin, out in the woods, near a town called Morris in Wyoming. We were going to be married, raise a family . . . It didn't happen. I never liked her going into town by herself. There was a lot of drifters, gunslingers, just like here, but she also had an independent streak. I admired that in her; I don't believe in putting a woman in a cage.

51

Well, to make a long story short, one day she rode into town . . . and never came back. She was raped and murdered on the way in. I don't know for a fact, but I heard it was John Brutus and some of his pack who killed her. Somebody said they overheard John Brutus bragging about it in a saloon in Morris. That somebody was later found shot dead when the law went to question him. They never found out, or I should say, they never brought to justice the men who raped and murdered her." Stone swallowed hard and his gaze narrowed.

"She . . . she wanted to be a teacher. She loved kids; she wanted a big family . . . When I started drifting again after she was murdered, I went back to San Francisco for a while. I grew up there. I was an orphan. I don't know . . . I've always wanted to do something with my life, something meaningful. I just never knew quite what. Since I'm pretty good with a gun, well, something just came to mind when I went back to my orphanage. They were talking about closing the place down, lack of money. This was maybe six months back. They said they could hold on for maybe a year. They needed about twenty thousand to keep the place running. I told them to hang in there, that I'd be back with the money. That's when I decided I'd go out and see if I couldn't find some justice in the world after all. So, what money I can collect for the heads of John Brutus and some of his bunch, it's not going into my pocket, not all of it. I'll take what I need to live on, of course. But most all of it'll be for the orphanage, sort of a . . . memorial fund for the woman I would've married."

Jessie stared at Stone, feeling a newfound respect for him. She looked away from his penetrating gaze, feeling her heart go out to him. She felt his pain; she felt his loneliness. Though she'd never had any children herself, she loved kids, and she respected what Stone wanted to do.

"How are you going to do it?" she asked him after a moment's silence. "I mean, how are you going to go about getting them?"

"At night. While they sleep. With a knife to their throats or a gun to their heads. They can come peacefully or they can go, resting in pieces. One by one."

"With all that money riding on their heads, I'm surprised no one's tried to collect the bounty before now."

"Well, at least no one who's lived to talk about it anyway. Besides, Brutus and his bunch are protected."

"What do you mean?"

"Law in this territory, they're owned by Max Haley. I'm talking about federal marshals. Heard a rumor the governor of this territory is buried so deep in Haley's pocket, he couldn't find his way out with both hands and a parade of lanterns. Not surprising, though. Max Haley has more money than God." Stone paused, then asked Jessie, "What about the girl who's with you—Christine? She seems real uncomfortable and scared. Something tells me she's not just along for the ride."

"She isn't," Jessie said, and told Stone how they had found Christine, what had happened to the girl's brother, and what they had done to the outlaws out on the desert.

Stone let out a soft whistle of admiration when Jessie recounted how she and Ki had left all six outlaws for the vultures; then he shook his head about the girl's brother. "She seems like a sweet kid. Sorry to hear what happened to her brother. Somebody finds those bodies out there, I guess I don't have to tell you you'd better be prepared to shoot your way out of here."

"Yeah" was all Jessie said.

For several moments, they sat in silence, Stone seeming lost in the past, while Jessie weighed her options. The buzzing of the fly filled the tight silence. What to do? Jessie wondered. Team up with Stone and take the town on, she, Ki, and the bounty hunter? Go their separate ways and do what each of them had to do?

Then she heard the jingle of spurs on wood beyond the door, lots of spurs. Suddenly, without warning, as she reached for her Colt, the door opened. Jessie and Stone bolted to their feet, fists wrapped around weapons, as the door banged against the wall.

They froze, a heartbeat before drawing iron, as a short gunslick with a black patch over his left eye held up one hand while the other was draped over his holstered six-shooter and said, "Easy, people! This is a friendly call."

Behind the one-eyed gunman, Jessie saw the hallway packed with a half dozen sweat-grimed, leering faces and rifles canted to shoulders. Despite what One Eye had told them, nobody looked all that friendly to Jessie.

"You know how to knock?" Jessie rasped.

"Sure," One Eye said, and chuckled. "But I was hoping to catch me an eyeful."

"If you had," Jessie said, tight-lipped, "I would've made sure you left completely blind."

"Why, you—"

"Shut up!"

Jessie recognized the familiar voice from Haley's Comet. A big shadow moved behind the pack in the hall. Slow. Bold. The gunpack parted. And, moments later, as the one-eyed gunman stepped into the room, a snarl still twisting his bearded face, John Brutus appeared in the doorway. Jessie felt her adrenaline race, as she saw Stone visibly tense at the sight of the man who might've raped and murdered the woman he'd loved.

"Mr. Haley wants a word with you," John Brutus told Jessie.

"About what?" Jessie asked, suspicious.

Brutus shrugged. "Didn't ask the man that."

"I hope it's not another business proposition," she said, glancing at Stone, "like the kind I've been getting since I arrived in Mr. Haley's fine town."

The one-eyed gunman chuckled, two flies picking at his sweat-slicked beard. "I hope it is, pretty as you are."

"Shut up, Hanks," Brutus growled at One Eye out of the corner of his mouth. "Shall we go see Mr. Haley?"

"Why not?" Jessie said, and moved toward Brutus.

Stone followed her, but Hanks spat, "Not you. Just Blondie."

"Both of 'em," Brutus said, boring a menacing stare into Stone.

For a second, Jessie would've sworn Brutus knew who and what Joe Stone was. She sensed a volatile rage building inside Brutus, about to erupt, but the big outlaw stepped aside and let them pass. Hanks made kissing sounds at Jessie as she moved out into

55

the hall. Jessie turned, her eyes cold, and saw Hanks staring at her ass.

"Sure hope it's bidness. I'll be first in line," Hanks chuckled, rubbing his crotch.

"You'll be the first to go, if you don't mind your manners," Jessie warned Hanks, "if you don't watch your eye."

As Hanks muttered, "We'll see about that," Jessie and Stone moved down the hall, surrounded by a phalanx of Haley's gunmen.

Inside the lobby of the Hotel Haley, Jessie found the man of the hour.

Max Haley was seated in a high-backed leather chair in the middle of the lobby. Two blond whores, wearing only white undergarments, were perched at Haley's feet like cats. Haley was dressed in a black suit and black tie, a bottle of brandy and a crystal glass on a small, round table beside him. He had a full head of white hair, blue eyes, and a square, clean-shaven jaw. He bared his pearly-white teeth in a wide smile as Jessie and Stone, surrounded by a dozen gunmen, moved toward him. He reeked of power and greed to Jessie. He looked clean, but he was as dirty as a pile of horse manure.

"Nice of you to come," Haley said. "I heard you and your rather odd-looking friend made yourselves quite the center of attention at the Comet."

Jessie checked the lobby. No sign of Jeb or any of the other gunhands she had seen earlier. Something didn't feel right to her; she smelled some kind of setup. She noticed several outlaws casting glances toward the doorway, as if expecting someone to arrive any moment. Suddenly, she was afraid for

Ki, her "rather odd-looking friend."

The lobby, she noticed, looking around, was big and plush, with velvet curtains hung above the plate-glass windows. Soft divans lined the walls; oil paintings hung everywhere, including a giant painting of Max Haley, looking smug and arrogant, staring out over the lobby from behind a long mahogany bar in the far corner of the room. Posh. Even the floor was carpeted, wall-to-wall, in a blood red.

Haley sat before Jessie like a king on his throne. He didn't wear a gun, but maybe, Jessie thought, he was hiding a derringer. Then again, Haley had surrounded himself with the most vicious guns east of the Mississippi, so he probably felt safe enough not to bother toting a weapon.

John Brutus moved to the bar, where he poured himself a shot of whiskey. Jessie felt, and smelled, the presence of Hanks, as One Eye stood almost right up on her backside. Stone stood like a statue, a lone gunman right beside him. The other gunmen fanned out, coming to rest in a half circle around Haley, their gazes fixed on Jessie and Stone.

Haley snapped his fingers. One of the whores stood, sliding a cigar from out of her garter and handing it to Haley, who ran his nose down the length of the stogie. "Ahh," he said, "nothing like the sweet smell of a woman's perfumed flesh on a good cigar." Scratching a match on the side of the chair, the first whore lit Haley's cigar while the other one poured him a glass of brandy. Haley puffed on his stogie, blew smoke, and took a long sip of brandy while the whores crouched at his feet again.

"You wanted to see me. What do you want?" Jessie asked.

"My, my, you are the little hellcat," Haley said, peering at Jessie through a cloud of smoke. "Pretty and sassy, just like I like my women."

Hanks snickered.

"I've heard so many flattering things about you, I just had to see you for myself," Haley went on, smiling, "and, I must say, you're every bit as beautiful as I was told. What's your name?"

"Jessie."

"Jessie." Haley squinted at Jessie. "Jessie what?"

"Just Jessie."

"All right. Just Jessie it is. How about you, stranger?" Haley said, eyeing Stone. "You've been hanging around my town for two days now. Just watching things. No women, no gambling for you. What's your story?"

"Just passing through," Stone said.

Haley grunted. "Uh-huh, well, if it turns out either of you are doing more than just passing through, well, you'll be buried in the hills in an unmarked grave. You can pass that on to your friend who I understand made himself quite the show. Why, just two weeks ago," he said, looking at Stone, "a couple of strangers told me they were just passing through, also. Turned out they were bounty hunters, imagine that. You get some free time, you might want to go pay your respects to them; they're buried in the hills. Right beside six other bounty hunters who thought they could come here and make a nice little profit in the past few months. You see," he said, smiling at Jessie, "I don't like it when strange faces ride into my town and start making noise. When they snap a man's arm like it was a twig, when they pull guns on my employees—in short, when they make my people look bad."

"I've got a feeling," Jessie told Haley, "your people can look bad without much help from us."

"I heard she had a smart mouth, Mr. Haley!" Hanks rasped. "I think she needs somethin' to plug it up!"

"Shut up," Haley told Hanks in a cold, level voice, his stare glued to Jessie. "I understand the people who run my business at the Comet made you an offer, which you so bluntly refused in your sassy hellcat style." Haley puffed on his cigar, then sipped his brandy. "That's okay. I'm not offended, at least not now. In fact, I'm glad you said no to them, now that I see what I'm seeing. You see, Jessie, I'm a man with a dream. My dreams will come true. And I always get what I want. I'm also, despite what you see, a lonely man, and a big man like myself without a good woman by his side . . . Well, the days are long and the nights are cold, shall we say. And when I say, *big*, Jessie, I mean big in more ways than one. What I want is one lucky lady by my side when all my dreams finally come true. A decent respectable lady. Not one of these," he said, glancing down at his whores, who, perched at his feet, looked up with traces of frowns. "They're okay for a spell, but they're just pets, something to ease some of the ache inside me. Something there to admire me and keep reminding me just how big I really am."

Jessie snorted. "And just what are your dreams, Mr. Big?"

Haley started to chuckle, then caught himself, scowled at Jessie for a second, and then finished chuckling. "Why, to own this entire Territory. And I will. I want to build the biggest town east of the Mississippi—no, I want it to be a city, the country's first city exclusive for gambling and prostitution, a city where the sun never sets, where the whiskey never stops flowing, where beautiful women never stop working their magic, where the card and keno games never end, where the roulette wheels never stop spinning. I'll build show palaces, with singers and bands and all kinds of entertainers from all over the country, from all over the world. I want this town to reach out into the desert for miles. I see it ablaze in light, with the biggest casinos and brothels ever built, buildings all trimmed in gold and silver, a sprawling American Sodom and Gomorrah, as the preacher-turned-pimp would say," he said, his eyes afire with ambition.

"Naturally, I don't see it quite like my preacher-pimp. I see Haley more like the Paris of the American West. I see hundreds and hundreds of working women here, all kinds of men, from a lowly cow-puncher, to a sheriff, all the way up to big business-men and politicians from back east. My town will be larger than life; my name will reach from coast to coast. I'm even going to build me a railroad—the Haley line. It'll run straight from New York City and Washington and San Francisco right here to my town." Haley paused, sucking on his cigar. "How about it, Just Jessie? You wanna ride with a sure winner? You wanna be *big*, too?"

Jessie said, "I like my life the way it is. And I'm afraid I've got other plans for myself."

"And just what sort of plans might they be?"

Jessie said nothing. Then, without warning, she felt a hand grab her rear and smelled Hanks right beside her as One Eye growled, "I suggest you answer the man, missie! I'll squeeze until you cry out!"

Jessie answered, all right, but it wasn't the answer anyone was looking for, or expected. Haley tensed, and a menacing scowl darkened the face of John Brutus, but before anyone could move or say anything, Jessie slapped Hanks's hand away and then backhanded him with a vicious crack to the chops.

"Bitch!" Hanks roared, and then his shout became a scream as Jessie clawed a viselike grip into his balls. "Aahhhhh!"

As Hanks crumpled to his knees, Jessie's Colt snaked from her holster. She shoved the gun barrel deep into Hanks's mouth and cocked the hammer.

Brutus, about to pour himself another drink, slammed the whiskey bottle down on the bar top and reached for iron as his outlaws started to fist gun butts.

But Joe Stone had already seized the moment, his Remington out and cocked, the barrel jammed into the ear of the gunslick beside him.

★

Chapter 5

"Don't anybody do something stupid all of you might regret!" Jessie warned the outlaws, as the whores gasped and cringed close to Haley, and the breath was seemingly all but strangled off in the throats of everyone in that lobby. "Mr. Haley, I suggest you keep your boys from getting itchy trigger fingers! Or I'll blow out this worthless scum-sucker's brains all over your lap. If I'm forced to do that, you never know who I might decide to shoot next."

Out of the corner of her eye, Jessie saw Stone keep his outlaw paralyzed with fear, the bounty hunter's gun jammed right into the scum's ear. Beneath her, Jessie saw Hanks's one good eye bulge in shock and terror as, on his knees, he gagged around the barrel of her Colt. Stooping some, she shoved the Colt's muzzle a good inch deeper down his throat and with her other hand squeezed his sac hard, making Hanks choke and squirm, his eye looking set to pop out of its socket in pain and terror. It was a crazy, reckless move, Jessie knew, but she'd acted on impulse, wanting to drive home the point that she wasn't a woman to be taken lightly, or taken advantage of; nor was she going to stand for some greasy lizard putting his hands on her whenever he damn well pleased. Normally, Jessie wouldn't and didn't outright humiliate a man, not even the lowest backshooter, and certainly not in a way that had shameful sexual overtones. But Hanks seemed the type who begged to be shamed, and she had felt a violent, overwhelming compulsion to oblige him. Hanks kept choking on iron, and when he swallowed, he couldn't help but suck the barrel.

And Jessie silently prayed she wasn't on the verge of a gunfight with maybe a dozen angry outlaws forced to watch one of their own humiliated. Again.

The tension in the air was thick, and all hell was about to break loose. If John Brutus and his outlaws drew now and started firing away, Jessie knew she and Stone would be buzzard meat. But the outlaws looked uncertain. Still, Jessie wondered how much longer she and Stone could hold them at bay before they said the hell with it and decided to watch Hanks get his brains blown out, just so they could regain their own animal sense of pride and power, unleash their own hyena's version of justice, and tear apart their prey, limb by limb, but with lead instead of hungry, frothing jaws.

"Everybody!" Haley boomed. "Be calm, don't move! The first man that draws, first man even squawks, I'll see to it personally he's castrated, then drawn and quartered!"

Brutus scowled at Haley.

"Don't look at me like that, John!" Haley rasped. "Your boy here, he asked for this. I invited her here as my guest and he insults me by putting his filthy hands on her. Far as I'm concerned, this jackal here, he can keep right on sucking that iron; it looks good in his mouth like that. Far as I'm concerned there, Just Jessie, you can blow his brains out."

Jessie glanced at Haley and saw that he was serious. She'd made her point, but cold-blooded killing didn't sit right with her.

Hanks tried to shake his head in protest, his eye begging for mercy, but Jessie made him choke some more on the iron and kept his sac in her viselike grip.

Gently, Haley set his brandy glass down. Looking calm, he stood. "I'm sorry about this varmint's lack of manners, Jessie, I truly am. I want to make it up to you." He walked up behind Hanks, looking Jessie square in the eye. He puffed several times on his cigar, its eye glowing cherry red. He blew a thick cloud of smoke down into Hanks's face. "Why don't you let me handle this?" he asked Jessie. "You, stranger!" he barked at Stone. "Put the gun back. Nobody's going to be shooting up my hotel; nobody's going to draw on you or Jessie here. You've got my word."

Stone hesitated, then uncocked the hammer on his Remington, which made a chilling sound in the angry silence. He lowered his gun away from the outlaw's head, holstered it, and took a long step back.

"Jessie. Now you," Haley said, and puffed on his cigar.

Jessie bore a cold stare into Hanks's lone, bulging

eye. "You ever lay a hand on me again, you ever look at me too long, I'll kill you. I won't even blink." As she uncocked the hammer, Hanks let out a muffled cry, horrified that the gun might go off. She slid the gun from his mouth and wiped the barrel off on his shirt. Then she released his sac.

No sooner had Jessie reholstered her iron, than Haley fisted a handful of Hanks's hair. Wrenching back on the outlaw's head, he thrust the glowing tip of his cigar toward Hanks's eye.

"Nooo!" Hanks screamed, but Haley held the cigar tip less than inch from the man's good eye. "Please, Mr. Haley, I didn't mean nothin'. I won't do nothin' like that ever again . . . Please . . ."

And Haley shoved the cigar into Hanks's mouth. Before Hanks could spit it out, Haley clamped his jaw shut and held him there, squirming on his knees.

"You're damn right you won't! I hope you don't have a problem with this, John," Haley called over his shoulder. "You and your people are on my payroll, but lately you been acting like I owe you something. Take a look at this sorry excuse for a man right here. I may have money, I may be up in years, but I can still hold my own. Call this a lesson in respect. Chew it up, Hanks! Eat it!" Hanks squeezed shut his eye, as a tear of pain and shame spilled down his bristled cheek. "You get out of line again, you won't have to worry about a woman shaming you. I'll shove a gun up your ass, right out in the street, in front of the whole town, and play some roulette with your yellow guts. I'll have everybody placing bets on when the hammer falls on the live round."

Jessie felt her heart skip a beat. Haley's rage, his cruelty, knew no bounds, that was obvious. What was also obvious to her was that, yes, Brutus and his gang did whatever Haley told them, allowed Haley to do whatever he wanted, even to one of their own. Haley, Jessie guessed, either paid them good, damn good, or he could turn the law in his pocket on them. Probably both. Just how much power did Haley wield? Jessie wondered. She intended to find out, but she would find out her way, not by becoming the plaything of Max Haley.

Hanks chewed up the cigar, as Haley kept his jaws clamped shut.

"You!" Haley snapped at the outlaw in front of Stone. "Open that door. I don't want this sorry sack of shit puking all over my carpet." The outlaw looked at Brutus, who nodded. "Swallow it, Hanks!" he bellowed at the one-eyed man as the other outlaw opened the double doors to the lobby. Hanks swallowed, his face twisted in agony. "Get up, get up!" Haley dragged Hanks to his feet. By the scruff of his neck, Haley pulled Hanks to the doorway. There, he slung him out of the lobby, kicking him square in the ass and sending him reeling across the porch, tumbling down the short flight of steps and out into the street. Haley slammed the doors shut, softening some the sound of the retching that ripped from Hanks's mouth. Haley spun on his heels and walked straight up to Jessie. In an icy voice, he told her, "I like you. I like your style. I really do. That's the only reason you and the stranger are going to walk out of here alive. But . . . you ever pull a gun on one of my people again, you'd better use it, and that goes for you, too, stranger,"

Haley rasped over his shoulder. "And I caught the implied threat, lady. Do not, I repeat, do not ever threaten me again unless you intend to kill me. You understand?"

Jessie held Haley's stare. She nodded. "I understand. Believe me, I understand."

Haley bore his stare into Jessie for another stretched second, then brushed past her and sat down. He snapped his fingers, and one of the whores refilled his brandy glass and handed it to him. He took a deep swig of brandy.

"Is that all, Mr. Haley?" Jessie asked.

"No." There was a moment of hard silence. "I want an answer."

"To what?"

"I need a queen to sit beside me on my throne. I want you," Haley told Jessie.

"I'm afraid, Mr. Haley," Jessie said, turning to leave, "you're going to have find yourself another bride."

"Hey!"

Jessie stopped beside Stone, turned, and looked back at Haley.

He was scowling, but the mean look faded into a wolfish grin. "Bride? Don't flatter yourself. It's not about marriage. I wouldn't marry you, or any woman. I like to keep my options open. What it's about is power. It's about dreams coming true. It's about having everything you could ever want."

"I have all I'll ever need, Mr. Haley. Right here inside me."

Haley chuckled. "You'll change your mind. I'd bet a life on it. And it won't be mine. In fact, before you walked in here, I already bet a life on it."

Jessie looked at Haley and felt ice tap down her spine. The ominous warning, no, the threat in his voice, didn't escape her. Something bad, she sensed, was about to happen.

Stone placed a gentle hand on her shoulder. "Come on."

Jessie broke Haley's laughing gaze and let Stone lead her out of there.

Ki dressed, as Christine lay curled up beneath the blanket like a kitten. With a dreamy look in her eyes, hugging the pillow, she watched Ki as he slid the scabbard and sword inside his sash and pulled on his vest.

"God, you're all man," Christine purred. "I never dreamed I could feel this good, want a man as much as I want you, Ki. I'd do anything for you. Anything."

Ki smiled at Christine and smoothed back his sweat-plastered black hair. Only moments ago, they had gone at each other again, with wild, reckless, fiery abandon. Ki was amazed at her stamina, the depth of her passion. For a near-virgin, she was a tigress in bed; her body could be wracked by one endless convulsing orgasm after another.

"You leaving?" she asked.

"For a little while. I'm going to check on Jessie. I can bring you up that steak, if you're hungry."

"I'm hungry," she said, grinning, "but not for food."

Ki heaved a breath, shook his head, and chuckled. He was spent, weak in the knees. "Let me get something in my belly first. Please."

"Okay. Since you said 'please.' Ki?"

"Yes?" he said, noting the fear in her eyes.

"I'm scared. I'd hate to see anything happen to you. Of course, that goes for Jessie, too. I won't forget what either of you have done for me. You'll be careful, won't you?"

"I can only promise I'll be as careful as this town allows me to be."

"I don't like the sound of that, but that's honest enough."

Ki turned away from Christine and was headed for the door, halfway across the room, when he sensed the presence of danger out in the hall. He stopped in mid-stride. Since he'd been in the room with Christine, he had heard the laughter and creaking springs in the rooms beside them, as whores coupled with johns. Now, as if those rooms had been cleared out, there was only silence. Dead silence.

Boots scuffed wood beyond the door.

"Ki, what's wrong?"

"Ssshhh."

The silence beyond the room was so thick, Ki could hear a man whisper, "Don't kill him. We were told to take him alive. Or it's our hides instead."

Ki dug out a *shuriken* and fisted the hilt of his *katana*. A heartbeat later, the door was splintered into flying wood shards. Two gunmen, with iron out and poised to shoot, burst through the door. One of the gunman was Bowlegs Kiley; the other one was Ollie.

Christine screamed, pulling the sheet tight to her breasts. "Ki!"

Ollie's face was twisted with feral rage. "Awright, you bastard, you can come peacefully . . ."

Ollie never finished his sentence.

Ki wasn't about to go peacefully or any other way. He sent the *shuriken* spinning through the air, a lightning flash of steel that impaled Ollie's upper arm. Screaming, hitting his knees, Ollie dropped his gun and clawed at the steel star embedded in his flesh.

Another blur of steel whirled through the air and sliced into Kiley's upper leg. He crumpled to the floor.

Ki unsheathed his sword. A gunslick Ki recognized as Crawford slid into the doorway.

And Ki became a human cyclone of fists and feet.

Beyond Crawford, he heard the familiar, angry voice of Jeb, as the man whose arm he'd shattered raged, "I want that fuckin' bastard. I don't care what we were told! I'll kill him! I want his ass all for myself!"

★

Chapter 6

Sure, it was a setup, Ki knew, but questions danced through the back of his mind: Why capture him and who had ordered it? Only one way to find out, he decided. Kick ass, and take no prisoners. They meant to take him alive for some reason.

All of them but Jeb.

Which gave Ki a deadly advantage, because he didn't have to leave any of them breathing. And since Jeb was hell-bent on disobeying whoever had given them their orders, Ki was going to make Jeb pay, painfully and dearly. Once and for all.

On the attack, Ki hammered a *mae-geri-keage*, a forward snapkick, off the tip of Crawford's jaw. There was a sound like a thunderclap, as Crawford's mouth snapped shut on tongue and teeth. The force of the blow lifted him off his feet and flung him back into Jeb, the severed tip of Crawford's tongue and bits of his broken teeth flying through the air behind a misty curtain of blood. Ki saw that Jeb's broken arm was in a sling, but a Colt .44 filled the gunslick's free hand, and he meant to use it. As Crawford slammed into Jeb and knocked him off-balance, the cocked hammer fell on Jeb's Colt, blasting a wild round that scorched past Ki's cheek and drilled into the ceiling. Jeb reeked of whiskey—to kill the agony in his arm, Ki figured. The injured gunslick's eyes were bloodshot and bleary, but the effects of liquor would be cleared by Jeb's mindless rage and burning desire for revenge.

Ki wasn't about to let any of these gunmen take their pound of flesh off him, or Christine. With savage determination, he cracked a backhand hammerfist into Kiley's nose, mashing it to bloody mush and dropping the bowlegged gunhand like a sack of potatoes. A *mawashi-kubi-geri*, a sweeping hook kick, and Ki floored Ollie, out for the count, sending broken teeth and bloody froth spraying from the gunman's shattered face.

Sword in hand, Ki surged through the doorway. Jeb wobbled to his feet, his gun hand shaking as he tried to draw down on the human hurricane that was Ki, but he hesitated and stumbled, forced to gather his senses as brain-searing agony from his shattered arm burned like a torch in his eyes. Out of the corner of his eye, Ki saw a shadow charge him. Lashing out with a kick, he lanced his foot deep into the shadow man's gut, doubled him over, and sent him reeling back down the hall, into the waiting arms of two other gunmen, who toppled to the floor behind the crushing weight of their buddy-in-ambush.

"I'll kill you, you goddam bastard!" Jeb roared. "You're dead, you shit!"

The sword was a flash of steel in Ki's hand as he drove the razor-sharp blade sideways. Because of the sideways angle, Ki had no choice but to send the blade slicing through the shoulder of Jeb's bad arm, when he would've rather taken out his gun hand. The blade of the samurai cut through enemy flesh like a hot knife through butter. A hideous shriek ripped from Jeb's lips as his severed, splintered arm thudded to the floor beneath a shower of crimson rain. Screaming at the top of his lungs, he toppled into the wall, horrified bulging eyes staring down at his dismembered appendage.

Ki sensed someone charging up behind him. He launched himself into a reverse spinning kick. Like stone cracking stone, the side of Ki's foot caught the gunman high on the side of his face, driving him off his feet and hurling him into the wall as if he weighed no more than a rag doll.

"I'll kill you!" Jeb screamed, tears of rage and pain streaming down his cheeks, blood spraying across the hall from the gaping hole where his arm used to be.

Ki was left with no choice but to deal death, as he saw Jeb's Colt again track his way. So he slashed Jeb's throat open, the tip of his *katana* a steely blur as it sliced across the gunman's neck. More blood geysered, but now crimson was spraying from the gruesome yawn across Jeb's throat. Jeb looked at Ki in horror and disbelief and dropped his gun, his hand grabbing at his sliced throat, thick arterial blood squirting through splayed fingers before he toppled, a full second later, facedown in a pool of his own spreading gore.

"Jesus God! That's enough, mister! Don't move

another muscle. Don't even twitch, or I'll blast you into a hundred pieces!"

Ahead, at the end of the hall, Ki, his vest, shirt, and face splattered with the blood of his enemies, saw Sheriff Doughty, who crouched and took aim with a Winchester .44 rifle.

The sounds of men moaning in agony cut the heavy silence.

"Ki!"

Out of the corner of his eye, Ki saw Christine, sheet wrapped around her naked body, jump off the bed. He held out a hand.

"Stay there," he told her.

He heard maybe a half dozen hammers click back on revolvers behind him.

Sheriff Doughty jacked the lever action on his Winchester. "Drop the sword, mister! And you jist keep your friggin' yap shut. I'll give the orders!"

Ki squatted, and gently, almost with reverence, laid the sword of the samurai on the floor.

"Git your hands up!" Doughty barked.

Ki put his hands up. A swarm of buzzing flies teemed over the dead and the mangled, picking at the free-flowing blood and sweat.

"You're under arrest, mister!"

"For what?" Ki asked.

"For what!? For murder!" Doughty growled.

Christine, ignoring Ki's advice, strayed out into the hall. "The hell he is, it was self-defense. They broke the door down and came in with guns drawn!"

"Shut up, girl!" Doughty roared. "The way I see it, it's murder, plain and simple. Marlin! Cuff 'em."

Moments later, Ki saw a tall, skinny deputy walk up beside him.

"You so much as blink, I'll drill ya!" Doughty warned. "Boys, he gets funny, you got my okay to fill 'im up with lead, make him dance a jig!"

As Deputy Marlin cuffed him, Ki heard a throaty chuckle behind him. Turning, he saw the preacher-pimp and Pluto standing at the end of the hall. They were surrounded by five of their painted ladies.

"We gotcha," Edwards laughed.

Stone loping beside her, Jessie was halfway down the street when she saw Ki shoved through the batwings of Haley's Comet.

"I knew it," she rasped through clenched teeth, running toward the saloon-brothel-casino. "Ki!"

"You keep your distance, missie!" Sheriff Doughty ordered, the muzzle of his Winchester jammed into Ki's spine, while a dozen gunmen surrounded Ki, the sheriff, and his deputy, who was carrying Ki's sword and vest stuffed with *shurikens*.

"Just what the hell do you think you're doing?" Jessie asked Doughty as she stopped a dozen feet short of the rolling phalanx ushering Ki across the street, toward jail.

"About time you did something around here, Sheriff!" someone cackled from the mob that had formed on both sides of the street. " 'Sides take the Man's money, and jack off while you wishin' you could bury yer face in some dirty pie and for free, I might add!"

"Shut your filthy, lyin' hole!" Doughty roared at the wiseass.

The mob laughed. They looked like a pack of hyenas to Jessie.

"Hey, I asked you a question!" Jessie snarled at Doughty.

"What the friggin' hell's it look like I'm doin' here, lady?" Doughty shot back. "I'm takin' your boyfriend here to jail for murder!"

"You're some sorry excuse for a lawman," Jessie told Doughty.

"You watch your mouth, lady," Doughty snarled. "I'll toss you behind bars, too!"

"I don't think that would go over too well with Mr. Big, Sheriff," Jessie said.

Doughty scowled at her, but said nothing. The truth stings, Jessie knew.

Ki looked at her. "They set me up, Jessie."

But she already knew that. Eyes hard, she turned and looked back at the Hotel Haley. No sign of Mr. Big, the mastermind behind the frame-up. She had a good mind to walk right into the lobby, thrust her gun under his chin, and make him release Ki, make Mr. Big small, make him beg for mercy, cut him down to his real size, reduce him to a shamed whelp with its tail between its legs. Then just shoot him and take on the whole goddam town. Without a doubt, she knew, there wouldn't be any justice for Ki. Except hanging justice. Behind her she saw John Brutus and a dozen of his guns slowly walking down the middle of the street. Their hands were draped over the butts of their guns. What the hell, she thought, were they going to shoot them down right there in the middle of the street? No, she decided, Haley was going to use Ki as his trump card. To make her, Jessie thought, his queen. The bastard had planned it all before she'd even left Stone's room.

Moments later, Jessie saw Brutus and his guns stop. Brutus looked her right in the eye and grinned. Victory.

78

"Jessie!"

Jessie turned, as Christine, fully dressed now, raced up to the heiress and the bounty hunter.

"What happened?" she asked Christine.

"Dirty sons of bitches," Christine snapped. "They bust in, guns drawn. They forced Ki to kill one of 'em, the one whose arm he broke earlier. It was clear self-defense, but they're calling it murder!"

"Not the way I saw it," Doughty called back, leading Ki up onto the boardwalk in front of his jail office.

"Not the way you saw it, or is it the way you've been paid to see it?" Jessie shot back.

"It's the way it is, lady," Doughty said, then pushed Ki through the doorway of his office. "Won't be any visiting hours for this one here either. Not until his trial."

"Trial," Jessie scoffed. "Just what are you going to do with him, Sheriff?"

"We'll let you know." Then Doughty vanished inside his office. The wall of gunmen fanned out, moving down the boardwalk. Their job was done.

Jessie saw Edwards and Pluto push through the batwings of Haley's Comet. Edwards was chomping on a cigar, all smiles.

"You ready to talk some business with the Man?" Edwards asked.

"It'll be a cold day in hell," Jessie answered.

Edwards shrugged. "You should lighten up, lady. Damn, I'm one of the last of the good guys in this town, a real gentleman. Easy to get along with, a real likeable sort of fella. Think I'll start wearing a white hat even. Think I'll start calling myself 'Gentleman Ed' from now on."

"You're mighty smug, pimp," Jessie said. "Your day's coming. And this wasn't your idea anyway, so don't try and play me for a fool."

"Not a fool, just a sucker. Want I should draw you a picture? Put *the word* in front of *sucker* for you?"

Jessie felt her hand twitch. Stone must've seen the murder in her eyes, because he took her by the arm and said, "Come on, Jessie, let's get out of the street. You, too, Christine. You better come with us."

Jessie looked back at Brutus, who was still grinning in triumph. If ever a town needed cleansing, she thought, if ever a place needed to be burned down to smoldering ash, this town was it. More than ever, she was determined to take Haley down— watch his body twitch in death throes as his dream of building the Paris of the American West went up in flames.

It was almost a full two hours since Ki had been tossed into jail, and Jessie was still seething with a deadly fury. They were now once again in Stone's room. Jessie saw Christine walk in behind the bounty hunter, who had gone to his horse to get his Winchester rifle. Stone closed the door, then canted the rifle up against the bed. The three of them had eaten steak, potatoes, and bread at a small saloon at the edge of town. It wasn't the Comet, but Jessie had seen the same kind of flesh-for-sale business going on in the eatery as she had witnessed at Haley's biggest whoring establishment. For the first time since they'd ridden into town, no one had bothered them while they had eaten; townsmen and whores had just cast the three of them knowing glances.

They were three now against a whole town, with the fourth behind bars.

"Got you two a room right next to me," Stone said. "If I sleep for a while, it'll be with one eye open. If they do come, they'll be in for a helluva fight."

Christine plopped down on the edge of the bed. She was sullen and angry. "Why? Why are they doing this?"

"Because," Stone said, moving to the window to check the street. "They want you. Both of you."

Christine still didn't understand. "But why?"

"At the risk of sounding crude," Stone said, "it's because you're . . . pretty and unsoiled. The powers-that-be see you as a top-dollar draw."

"Can't tell you how flattered I am," Christine said huffily.

"It's the way of bad men," Stone said. "They see something they want, they'll take it, no matter what they have to do. It's a sick pride thing. Like the preacher-pimp might say if he weren't one of them, this town and its people are Lucifer and his angels rising up against God 'cause they want to be God, then falling and finding out the only place they're fit to rule is Hell. The only place Haley, Brutus, and his cutthroats can rule is right here. Hell. And we're up against the Devil, you can believe that."

"What he's saying is true, Christine," Jessie said, standing next to Stone, having watched from the window as the mob dispersed for the casino, for a night of heavy drinking, whoring, and gambling. The sun was beginning to set, shadows stretching over the town. "They set Ki up. They're using him to get you and me."

81

"Well, night's coming," Stone said, tight-lipped. "And it's going to be a hot night here in Helltown."

Jessie saw the fire in his eyes. "You've got something in mind. What?"

"I'm thinking how we're going to get the Devil to dance to our tune."

"Well, we have to do something," Christine said. "We can't just leave Ki in jail like that. They could drag him out into the street any minute now and lynch him."

"No," Stone said. "They won't do that. They'll come here first and make an offer."

Jessie knew Stone was right, that Ki was safe, at least for the moment. Haley had his ace in the hole to get what he wanted. But they needed a plan. They had to break Ki out, Jessie knew, soon, and then all hell was surely going to break loose.

"Christine," Jessie said, "I need to talk to Mr. Stone for a minute. Why don't you go get some sleep? Lock the door to your room. We'll be right here. They may not come with spurs on this time, but we'll be ready just the same."

She hesitated. "But . . . okay. I don't know that I can sleep any, but I'll try. You two put your heads together and come up with an idea to spring Ki, you'll let me know, right? I'll be in on it, right?"

Jessie nodded. "You'll know."

"I hate it. I hate this town," Christine said, standing. "I don't think I can wait long. I can't stand the thought of Ki behind bars like that, helpless, God only knows—"

"Christine, you've got to be patient," Jessie told her.

Christine's face stayed flushed with anger and

impatience. Stone walked her out the door and to her room. While she waited for Stone to return, Jessie kept watch on the street. There was no sign of Brutus or the sheriff. All right, it was wait-and-see time, before one of Haley's vultures came to her with an offer they were sure she couldn't refuse. She turned as Stone came back into the room. He closed the door.

There was a long moment of silence, a heavy silence that Jessie felt weighing on her. She felt Stone move up on her from behind.

"I've got a plan, but we're going to have to wait a while, until a lot of these people get involved in the night."

"Just what . . ." Jessie turned and found herself suddenly staring deep into Stone's penetrating blue eyes. She froze, mesmerized by what she saw in his eyes. Just as she'd seen the first time, there was a toughness in those eyes, but a hint of compassion; this was a man who could be mean but also gentle and understanding. He had the eyes of a killer, but there was heart and soul in those eyes, the eyes of a man who had traveled a dark and lonely road, a man alone, a man who could stand up and be counted when you needed him most. And once again, she felt her breath lock up in her throat, felt her stomach quiver. Stone placed a gentle hand on her face. A part of her wanted to pull away from his touch; another part, a bigger part of her, wanted this man like she'd wanted no man in quite some time. His touch felt cool but warm on her face, soothing, gentle. What little bit of hardness was in his eyes melted away, replaced by a fiery hunger. He pulled her a little toward him, and she brushed up against his crotch.

He was ready, hard as pistol iron, she saw. And she almost gasped at the size of the massive bulge in his crotch as it strained to break free of his pants.

"Stone . . . Joe . . . I don't know if this is the time . . ."

"Ki will be all right for now," Stone said and kissed her on the mouth.

It was a soft kiss, like butterflies fluttering over her lips, and Jessie felt a fire stir in her belly. His lips caressed her with tenderness. They kept kissing, and Jessie wanted to keep kissing this man forever. She sensed the savagery behind the gentle mask, the devil behind the angel. She was burning to feel him in her.

"Let's take this moment, Jessie. Let's live for right now. None of us ever knows what's going to happen tomorrow. I'm in this with you. We'll get Ki out; we'll take on this whole town together."

She believed him. With all her heart, body and soul, she kissed him with hunger. Jessie felt her mouth open wider, felt her heart beating faster with want and anticipation, felt her knees weaken. The way he kissed her, slow, soft, was drawing her, it seemed, into his own fire, closer and closer to his huge hardness. She felt a tingle between her legs, felt herself moistening with desire. Gently, he cupped her breasts, massaged her nipples. Jessie felt her nipples harden, felt the wetness become a raging fire between her legs.

"Lock the door," she said, pulling away from him. And as Stone did so, and wedged a chair under the knob, Jessie undressed. Moments later, as she stretched her long, supple, creamy nakedness out on the bed, Stone was naked himself.

He settled on top of her. She looked at the corded, rippling muscles of his body. He was a beautiful hunk of man, she decided, and saw his big, thick cock thrusting up at her, reaching all the way up and past her belly. She took it in her hand, kissing Stone, feeling the hardness of his pole and his knotted washboard stomach muscles brushing against her belly. Pushing him up a little off her, she rubbed the massive head against her and felt the blood pulsing through Stone's iron-hard manhood. Jessie's breath shot out of her mouth, faster and faster with craving for him; she felt herself on the verge of exploding. Stone kept teasing her, making her gently rub his head on her slippery wet, pink lips. She pulled her legs back, clawing her fingers into the rock-hard muscles of his shoulders. He kissed her neck, then sucked her breasts, licking her nipples. She couldn't stand it any longer; she thought she was going to scream with pleasure, demand he take her. Then, finally, she felt him enter her, slowly. Deeper and deeper he slid into her. Jessie moaned, cried out. She felt so filled; he went up so deep into her womb she thought she would be split in half. Her moans became a soft whimper, as she matched Stone's easy rhythm, wanting it to last forever.

"You're beautiful, Jessie," Stone whispered into her ear. "You're the most beautiful woman I've ever seen."

Jessie felt a smile tug at her lips, a smile that felt as if it hurt her face, as he plunged even deeper, withdrew, then drove himself into her, again and again. This man was a stallion, a studhorse in human disguise. She rocked and thrust herself against him, feeling herself building toward orgasm as he kept kissing her neck, rubbing her breasts. She locked her legs around him, locked a kiss on his mouth, as he bucked, in and out, crushing her round, smooth-skinned behind into the mattress. Jessie felt the fire sear every nerve ending in her body, and then she felt herself erupt with orgasm. The pleasure kept bursting through her. Her head felt light, faint; she felt herself falling into her own soul as she cried out. Then she felt him explode in her, drenching her womb, deep, with a wet fire that cooled her belly. He kept shooting into her, juicing her, one big spurt after another.

Finally, he kissed her on her hot mouth with the same tenderness as the first kiss. She wrapped her arms around his neck, mashing herself into him. He slid himself out of her, his long, heavy meat hanging between her legs.

Jessie heaved a sigh. She knew she'd still be feeling him inside her long after the night was a memory. She touched his sweaty face and smiled. She felt warm and fulfilled. But behind the glow in her eyes the fire still burned. Soon, real soon, she knew, she'd be wanting this man again, this studhorse in human form.

★

Chapter 7

Ki seethed behind bars, his hands clasped between his legs as he sat on the iron-base cot mounted to the brick wall. Sheriff Doughty and his skinny deputy sat behind their desks. Ki's sword and vest were piled in the far corner, beneath the rifle rack. Night had fallen over Haley, and a kerosene lantern bathed the jail office in deep shadows. So far, no one had come to see Ki. Not the conspirators, not Jessie, but Ki knew Doughty wasn't about to let the beautiful heiress pay him a visit. Doughty wanted to keep him alone and vulnerable to whatever whoever had in mind for him and Jessie.

And Ki knew what that was. Jessie and Christine's flesh for his hide. Haley, the pimp, the law, the whole damn town, was in it, and against them.

Doughty hadn't volunteered any information about anything. In fact, he hadn't said two words to Ki since tossing him in jail hours ago. Ki had asked questions, but had been told to keep his mouth shut.

He tried another tactic. "You're dirty, Sheriff. Your town's as dirty as an outhouse. You're swimming in shit, and you're going to drown in your own shit. You're a fly picking at a stallion for a few drops of lather. You're a snake that needs to be stepped on." Ki kept taunting. "You've sold out, sold your badge and your soul. How can you stand looking at yourself in the mirror? What do you see, Sheriff, when you shave in the mirror? A big pile of shit?"

Doughty looked at Ki with a level eye, lifted his legs off his desktop, and stood. He chuckled. "Tough talk from a man sittin' there with the threat of a noose hanging over his head."

"What are we going to do with this one, Sheriff?" Deputy Marlin asked.

"Sit on 'im. For now. The Man and his boys are heading out before dawn for their final piece of business. We'll know somethin' before then."

Ki didn't like the sound of that. The fuse on the dynamite of this situation, he thought, was burning low. Time was moving on into something sinister for him and Jessie and Christine. But he figured since he hadn't seen or heard from Jessie, she was planning something. Had to be. And he had to be ready to go, fight like hell, if she was planning on breaking him out.

"Bastard's real tricky with his feet, real mean with that sword of his and them throwing stars in his vest, too," Marlin groused. "Sliced poor Jeb's arm off, sliced his throat as easy as you or me would spit. Surprised Haley hasn't let ol' John Brutus string him up by now, or at least bust him up good."

"Shut up, Deputy," Doughty growled. "You ain't

bein' paid to think for the Man. Screw this waitin' around. I'm goin' across the street," Doughty announced, hitching up his gunbelt. "Grab me a few beers, maybe indulge myself in one of the pimp's trollops. I'll be gone a while, so don't nod off, Marlin. Come back, find you asleep, I'll slap you silly jist like a woman."

Marlin grunted a curse as Doughty left the jail office. As soon as the sheriff was out of sight, Marlin opened a drawer in his desk. He took out a whiskey bottle, uncorked it, and sucked down a healthy swallow.

"Nod off, he says," Marlin grumbled to himself. "Tired of people like him talkin' to me like I'm some kinda green cowpoke snotnose."

But, as the minutes passed, and Marlin swallowed down a quarter of the bottle of whiskey, his eyes began to close, his head lolling forward. Beyond the plate-glass window, Ki noticed, there wasn't much activity on the street, hardly a shadow of a gunslick moving on the planks. The whole town would've seemed deserted if he hadn't heard the wild bursts of laughter from inside Haley's Comet.

Then Ki spotted a shadow, a small figure just outside the window. He tensed, then recognized Christine as she quietly opened the door. Ki felt his heart race as he looked at Marlin, afraid the deputy would snap out of it. But a snore buzzed from his mouth. Christine watched Marlin, checked behind her, then stepped into the office. She had a good-size rock in her hand. Ki gave her high marks for guts. Damn, but if she was caught now . . .

Bold as brass, she walked right up to Marlin and cracked the deputy over the head with the rock. His

89

hat flew, and he crumpled out of his chair and hit the floor, out cold.

"Christine, forgive me for asking a stupid question, but just what the hell do you think you're doing?" Ki asked.

Christine plucked the key off Marlin's gunbelt. She smiled at Ki and looked as if she were actually enjoying herself.

"I couldn't wait any longer. I was worried about you, Ki," she said, slipping the key into the hole and opening the cell door.

Ki looked out the window and saw nobody within sight of the office. "Where's Jessie?"

"With that Mr. Stone. They said they had some kind of plan, but like I said, I was just sitting around my room. I was scared these people might just kill you. You've got to leave town, Ki, run!"

"Running isn't my way," Ki said, and took the gunbelt off Marlin, fastened it around his waist, and then took back his sword and vest.

"They'll kill you, they see you in town."

Ki stopped for a second and stared at Christine in the shadows. She had a point.

"All you have to do, Ki, is get out of town and wait for a while in the hills. I'll go tell Jessie what I did. She can come find you."

"What do you think's going to happen to you and Jessie when they find I've escaped? Think things through."

"No. You leave."

Before he could say anything further, Christine was out the door.

"Damn it, you're stubborn as a mule, girl."

Ki was about to bolt after her, but then he saw

some gunmen moving toward the Comet from the other end of the street. If he strayed out into the open now, he'd be in for a fight, plus he'd be putting Jessie and Christine at further risk. Christine was right, he acknowledged begrudgingly. He should get out of town, lay low, and wait for Jessie to come and round him up. Hope that Sheriff Doughty found himself a trollop and stayed put for a while. And then what? Playing it by ear was over, thanks to Christine's reckless daring. These people were serious, deadly serious.

With rope, Ki tied Marlin's hands and feet. He tore the deputy's shirt off, then stuffed a sweat-grimed shred of cloth in Marlin's mouth. The deputy moaned, blood trickling down the side of his face. Ki put his lights back out with a short, slashing right to the jaw.

Then he hit the back door running. With one forward snapkick, he shattered the lock on the door, hurling wood splinters out into the night. Ki checked the area behind the buildings. Nobody in sight. No, running was not his way, but he wasn't running, he knew; he was merely waiting.

For all hell to break loose.

Ki melted into the night and forged beyond the outskirts of Haley.

Naked, in a sheen of soft yellow light from the kerosene lamp on the nightstand, Jessie sat in the big copper tub Stone had rented and carried up to the room from the downstairs lobby. She needed to relax, calm herself, do some thinking about the plan. She figured a quick, hot bath was as good a way as any right then to sort through things, while they waited for the people of Haley to involve themselves in the night, as Stone had put it. Bucket in hand, Stone sloshed into the tub the last of the hot water he'd hauled up from downstairs. His Winchester and Jessie's Colt were right beside the tub. Jessie soaped her creamy ivory-white shoulders and arms, the hardened nipples of her firm, succulent breasts resting on the water. The hot water felt good, soothing on her skin.

"I almost feel guilty about enjoying myself this much," she told Stone. "Ki rotting in jail . . ."

"Just a little while longer, Jessie, while these people get drunk and pair off, then we'll do it."

They had gone over the plan. Jessie liked it.

"You mean set fire to the Comet," Jessie said, grinning, "then go bust Ki out, slip into the hills, and start picking them off with rifles from a distance . . . like flies."

"You don't like it?"

"I do, and I don't. Sure, I want to see this town burn, but I want to be able to look Max Haley right in the eye when I pull the trigger."

"When that fire spreads, and it'll spread fast, dry as this timber is, and when Haley's running around the street, screaming like a demon, you'll see him. He's all yours. Whatever it takes to get him, you can have him, you have my word. And if they even get a chance to come after us, they'll have to come to us. We'll drop them, one by one."

"It's crazy, but the more I think about it, the more I like it."

Stone peeled off his shirt. "The more I think about you, Jessie, the more I like you. And the more I'm around you, the more I want you as a woman, like no woman before."

She looked up as Stone bent over her. He took the soap out of her hands and began gently washing her back.

"You check on Christine?"

"Damn," Stone grinned, "I knew I forgot something. I guess my mind was wandering."

"Don't let it wander later."

"Then let me let it wander now."

"That sounds like the beginning of a song, Joe. Are you a frustrated poet?" Jessie asked, a warm smile on her lips.

"Just a man."

"Isn't that the truth."

He soaped up her breasts, kneading her slippery nipples. Jessie moaned and shut her eyes, enjoying the soft touch of his strong hands on her skin. Then she felt Stone's mouth on her neck. Within moments, the fire spread through her belly again, quickly spreading between her legs until she felt as slippery as her soapy breasts, until she felt the tingle coursing up and down her spine like little pinpricks. The man's kisses, she thought, were like magic; they made her instantly want him. She reached over the edge of the tub, felt his crotch, and found him hard again.

"Stand up," she said. As he stood, Jessie unbuckled his pants and pulled them down. She took his huge organ in both hands, her mouth hot and watering with desire as she stared at its size. She put her full, ripe lips on the massive head, and Stone let out a soft groan as she stroked him with hand and mouth, swallowing as much of him as possible, slicking his shaft with her hungry mouth, roving wet lips, and darting tongue. Then she kissed his cock, while gently squeezing his sac.

"This could be considered a lethal weapon," she purred. "It's so big you could fit it in a rifle scabbard."

Stone put his hand on the back of her head, eased her out of the water, and helped her out of the tub. He kissed her, as she kept stroking the length of him with her hand, pulling it, twisting it gently, craving him again. It was so hard, it wouldn't bend a fraction of an inch. This was a man, this was all man, she thought; it would be a long, long time— no, she would never forget this man named Stone, this man made of stone.

"You're right," she breathed between kisses, as Stone ran his lips up and down her neck, rubbing her breasts, slippery with soap. "Tomorrow might not come. Let's take the moment . . ."

He reached down in the tub and picked up the soap. He eased Jessie down onto her knees and rubbed the soap on her pink lips. He got behind her and pitched the soap back into the tub. Dropping to her hands, Jessie felt her knees quiver with excitement as he slowly penetrated her from behind. She moaned. The irritation of the soap and the tight friction of her vagina accepting his size made her hurt but feel pleasure at the same time. Once again, she felt him go in so deep, so slow, so gentle, as if he were teasing her with each piercing, splitting inch, her breath locked up in her throat. Her heart, her soul, her flesh, burned for Stone.

Crouched behind her, he spread her firm, creamy-smooth cheeks, then began driving, thrusting deep into her. She slammed her butt back into him, demanding the whole huge length and girth of him, trying not to scream out as he split her, his big balls slapping her ass. She gnashed her teeth, her head swaying her coppery blond hair wet with water and sweat, swinging over her shoulders. She felt him rubbing her nipples, kneading her cheeks. Then, as if she weighed no more than a feather, he scooped her up in his big muscular arms. In one swift motion, he rolled beneath her, keeping her impaled on him. Jessie squatted over him, spread her legs as wide as they would go, and rode him, grinding herself up and down on his shaft, digging her hands into his chest, into muscles that felt as if they'd been carved out of granite. She writhed in a frenzy, feeling herself once again building to ecstasy, fiery waves of pleasure coursing through her. She squeezed her eyes shut, as she felt his strong hands spreading her ass wide. Then she cried out, as the orgasm suddenly, violently, ripped through her body, lasting longer, making her feel more faint, than the first time.

She slid off of him. She couldn't help herself; she wanted him in her mouth. She sucked him, stroked him with a fury. She felt him tighten, shudder, then explode, spurting hot semen deep into her mouth. She left her mouth on him for long seconds after he finished erupting, tasting him, enjoying his shivering in her mouth. Sighing, a smile of contentment on her lips, she laid her head on his stomach. Gently, she kept stroking him. Finally, he began to shrink in her hand. She kissed his balls, holding his big, limp meat in her hand.

"Oh, I could do this all night with you, Stone. But I think we'd better get dressed. Any more pleasure has to come after business from here on."

Stone nodded in agreement. "I'm just grateful we weren't interrupted. At least I would've died with a smile on my face."

Smiling, Jessie stood, toweled herself dry, then dressed, as Stone also slipped into his pants and shirt and put his boots on. She felt weak in the knees, light-headed. She wanted to savor the soreness, the ghost of him in her.

It didn't happen for Jessie, as grim reality shattered the moment.

Suddenly, before Jessie or Stone could arm themselves, the door exploded behind a thunderous kick.

"Move and the bitch here dies!"

Jessie froze. A half-dozen shadows with iron drawn burst into the room. One of the gunmen had an arm locked around Christine's throat, a revolver, hammer cocked, jammed against her head.

"Almost caught 'em with their pants down, Big John," one of the outlaws laughed.

And John Brutus rolled into the room and strode right up to Stone.

"Blink, asshole, you're dead," Brutus snarled at Stone. Then he swung a roundhouse right that hammered the bounty hunter's jaw and dropped him on his back.

Chapter 8

"Mighty damn stupid of your girl here," Brutus told Jessie, "to go and set your friend free."

Stone was on his knees, shaking the cobwebs from his head, as the room filled with gunmen.

"I'm sorry, Jessie," Christine cried. "I didn't listen to you, I should've waited but I couldn't . . ."

Brutus wheeled and backhanded Christine across the mouth.

Gunmen swooped in and hauled up Jessie and Stone's weapons.

"Now you've gone and forced Mr. Haley's hand, Sweet Cheeks," Brutus said to Jessie. "You ride with us, or you can die right here. Up to you. That's straight from Mr. Big, as you called him. One of ya, check her over good, make sure she ain't carryin' a little pocket pistol."

Jessie tensed as a leering gunman patted her down. "Watch yourself," she warned him in an icy voice as his hands started to stray toward her breasts. Then he found her derringer behind her belt buckle, grinned in triumph, and tossed the small weapon to Brutus, who caught it and put it in his pants pocket.

Another gunman was rifling through Stone's saddlebag, his jacket. His eyes widened as he pulled out the Wanted posters and handed them to Brutus.

"Just like I suspected," Brutus said, an ugly smile twisting his face as he looked through the Wanted posters. "Damn, they only want ten thousand for me? Only two thousand bonus for me dead? I'm insulted," he said, then laughed and kicked Stone in the face. Brutus struck a match and torched the Wanted posters. He held them in his hand for a long, dangerous moment, eyes glowing against the fire; then he pitched them into the tub, where they sizzled and smoked.

"Okay, Bounty Hunter," he said, "now I'm going to have some fun with you." Brutus launched a kick at Stone's face, but Stone caught his boot. Driving himself off the floor, Stone flung Brutus by the leg, up into the air, hurling him back into two of his men. As all three outlaws tumbled to the floor and Stone pivoted, cracking a vicious lightning right off the jaw of the outlaw who had pulled out his posters, Jessie started to charge the gunman beside her.

"Do it, bitch!" Jessie heard someone roar from the shadows. "And this one dies! Her blood'll be on your hands!"

Jessie froze. There seemed no way out; they would kill Christine if she fought back, Jessie knew. Three gunmen marched behind her, Colts cocked and aimed at the back of her head. Looking across the room, Jessie saw the one-eyed gunman she had humiliated earlier at the Hotel Haley, Hanks, with a Winchester aimed at Stone.

"You dirty bastard!" Brutus snarled, charging off the floor, fists clenched. "I'll bust you up!"

Stone hammered a right off Brutus's jaw, snapping the big outlaw's head back. Then Hanks swung his rifle butt at Stone's head from the deep shadows and cracked him over the back of his skull. Stone faltered, but didn't drop. He wheeled and kicked Hanks square in the nuts. The rifle fell from the outlaw's hands as Hanks clutched his punished sac and hit his knees, a long, low whimpering sound ripping from his mouth.

"Don't anybody shoot this bastard, no matter what!" Brutus raged, bulling in toward Stone, thunderclapping a right off Stone's jaw.

Jessie wanted to do something to help Stone, but she didn't dare move, knowing the outlaw holding Christine would surely kill her, that the gunman's eyes were burning through the shadows, looking right at Jessie, waiting for her to try something. No, she decided, she didn't dare go on the attack.

Four outlaws crushed in on Stone. Rifle butts and fists and feet pummeled him senseless. But Stone fought back with raw fury and courage, throwing fists into the wall of moving flesh, to crack jaws and slash cheeks. He fought on for a full half minute, bouncing outlaws off the wall, blood, sweat and spit flying from his mask of savage determination. Then the force of more numbers, as two other outlaws joined in, beat Stone to the floor. They kicked and pounded Stone for several moments, which felt like an eternity for Jessie.

"Stop! You're gonna kill him!" Christine wailed.

"Shut up, you little bitch!" the gunman holding Christine barked into her ear.

"Get 'im outside!" Brutus growled, driving a kick into Stone's ribs. "Take these bitches with ya, too!"

Jessie, adrenaline racing through her, afraid they were going to kill Stone, let herself be marched out of the room. She watched, helpless, as Brutus and his outlaws kicked, shoved, and punched Stone down the short hallway. Then Brutus drove his boot into Stone's ass and sent him tumbling down the stairs. Brutus laughed, descending the steps. Stone rolled up at the foot of the stairs. Unwavering gun muzzles tracked him, as the outlaws rolled up on him. With guns trained on them from behind, Jessie and Christine were ushered down the steps.

They kept pummeling Stone, through the lobby and out into the street. Jessie saw the blood streaming in thick gummy strands from his nose and mouth as he wobbled, then took a swing at an outlaw and cracked his jaw. She was sure they were going to kill him, and silently prayed for a miracle. Then, as she and Christine were led out into the street, Brutus dropped Stone with a right and loomed over him.

Surrounded by gunmen, Jessie saw a dozen shadows on horseback slowly ride from the direction of the Hotel Haley. Leading the pack, as yellow kerosene light burning from the boardwalk washed over the mounted mob, was Max Haley. Other outlaws on foot guided riderless mounts down the street behind him. Dozens of onlookers watched from the gloomy shadows of the boardwalks. A whore clapped and squealed with delight at the sight of Stone's beating.

Haley guided his mount close to Brutus. He grinned at Jessie, as he snapped his fingers and a mount was walked toward her by a gunman. "Get on, Just Jessie."

"I get the other one, Mr. Haley. It was a trade-off. Fair's fair."

Jessie recognized the pimp's voice as he called out from the mob across the street. She realized that she had no choice but to go with Haley, as more guns were cocked and leveled at her. And she wanted to go. Haley was up to something, and she wanted to know what that was. And where was Ki? she wondered. No doubt, she believed, he would not show himself now, outnumbered as they were, but he would follow wherever Haley was taking her.

"Leave that one," Haley told the gunman holding Christine, "for the pimp. That was our deal."

Brutus fisted a handful of Stone's hair and shook him like a dog. "You know, I thought I recognized you from somewhere, Bounty Hunter. It's coming back to me now. Up north, Wyoming way. You had a little cabin in the woods, didn't you?" His smile was ugly. "Had a little woman, too. Yeah, it's all coming back to me. Remember it like it was only yesterday. I'll tell ya, Hunter, she died with a smile on her lips."

Jessie saw the murderous rage burn through Stone's eyes. He tried to stand, fists clenched, but Brutus hammered a chopping right off his jaw and dropped him in the dirt. Brutus stood and grinned at Haley.

"So finish him," Haley said.

"No. Call this a lesson in respect, Mr. Haley."

"He comes back, he'll be coming back for you," Haley pointed out.

"He won't be coming back. I want him to live with a few memories. He's got a Wyoming memory, and now he's got a Haley memory. He knows now not to screw with John Brutus. By chance, if he's stupid enough to come after me, I'll leave him worse than this, worse than dead. Sometimes, you take away the pride of a man like this one, he's worse off than bein' dead already."

"If you're finished, we've got business, John," Haley growled.

"Get him on his horse. Give him back his guns, too," Brutus said, chuckling. "What the hell, huh? Maybe he thinks he is tough enough. If he is, I wanna see it."

Two outlaws hauled Stone off the ground, draped him over his saddle, hooked his gunbelt around his saddle horn, and sheathed his Winchester. Blood poured from Stone's mouth and rolled down his mount's belly. Then an outlaw slapped the horse's flanks, yelling. The animal bolted and raced out of town, heading west, with Stone clinging to the saddle. Jessie watched as the horse with Stone bucking in the saddle vanished from sight, racing up the rise that led west out of Haley. She felt a short moment's victory. Brutus had chosen not to kill him; he was arrogant enough to believe Stone had learned a lesson in respect. Could prove, Jessie thought, knowing what kind of man Stone was, to be the worst mistake John Brutus had ever made. She knew Stone would be back. Joe Stone had a lot more than just pride. He had balls; he had heart. In a fair fight, he could take any man there, by hand or gun.

"Jessie? I do believe I asked you to saddle up," Haley said. "Please, don't make me get ugly, darlin'."

Slowly, Jessie mounted the horse. Moments later, Brutus and another two dozen guns either mounted the horses that had been led down the street, or unhitched mounts from railings and climbed into the saddles. Okay, Jessie thought, something very serious was in the works here, everybody looked like they were headed out for war. What was going on?

"Jessie!"

Jessie watched as Christine was dragged across the street and flung to the ground at the feet of Edwards.

"What happens to her?" Jessie asked Haley.

"Why, she goes to work for Mr. Edwards," Haley answered. He reined his mount around.

"What about the other one, the one she let loose out of my jail?"

Jessie saw Sheriff Doughty roll up out of the dark, a scowl on the dirty lawman's face.

"Not a problem," Haley said. "You want him, you can go up in the hills after him."

Sheriff Doughty didn't look anxious to take Haley up on that offer.

Cold fear gripped Jessie, as Haley, Brutus, and the small army of gunmen reined their mounts around.

The thunder of pounding hooves led Ki to the far northwest edge of the rise. Since Christine had busted him free of jail, he had been circling Haley to the north, waiting, watching for any sign of Jessie.

He'd found her, all right, but it had been too late to do anything for her by the time the outlaw pack hit the streets, kicking and punching Stone.

Now, as maybe three dozen outlaws on horseback, kicking up a wall of swirling dust in their wake, rode up the east rise and vanished into the night, with Jessie as a hostage, Ki knew he was alone in a new kind of fight against the town, against Brutus and his cutthroats.

Alone, that was, until he saw the horse with its limp rider slung headfirst over the saddle. Stone.

Running along the west ridge, Ki cut an angle toward and ahead of the mount. On a dead run, he grabbed the horse by the reins, pulled down, and rode the mount to a stop. Stone toppled out of the saddle and hit the ground. For a long moment Ki thought the man was dead, as he stared down at Stone's bloody mask. Then Stone moaned. Ki watched the lip of the rise for any sign of movement. No one came.

The big guns had left Haley. That piece of business the sheriff had mentioned.

Ki grabbed the canteen off Stone's mount. Bending over Stone, as the bounty hunter peered up at Ki through swollen, cracked eyelids, Ki gently washed some of the blood and dirt off his face.

"Easy," he told Stone, as he held the canteen to the man's bleeding lips. Stone used the first mouthful of water to spit out blood.

"Jessie," Stone croaked.

"They took her."

"Where . . . where are they going?"

"I'm not sure, but when I was behind bars, I heard the sheriff say Haley and his bunch were leaving town for a final piece of business."

Stone struggled to sit up on an elbow. He drank more water. He handed the canteen to Ki. Ki wiped the nozzle off, then drank. The tepid water seemed to renew Stone's strength and determination as it hit his belly.

Stone groaned. "They busted me up . . . good . . . I don't think anything's broken . . ."

"Take it easy."

"No time. Only one way to find out about their business, Ki, and that's to march right down there. I'm going to show Brutus just how stupid he was to let me live. I'll catch up to him."

"No. We'll catch up to him."

"Hey! You up there, Ki!"

Startled, Ki swung his head toward the ridge. Crouching, he moved to the edge of the rise. There, he hit his belly and looked down into the valley. A big shadow stood in the middle of the street. He recognized the voice of the pimp's muscle, Pluto.

"If you can hear me, listen good! We've got your girl, Christine! Sweet thing, she sure is! I mean the boys in the Comet are damn near droolin' to get a taste!"

Ki felt his blood boil with rage.

"Now, you want, you can come on down, we can work somethin' out! You see, Mr. Edwards lost some money when you snapped that asshole's arm. He'd like it back! I understand the sheriff, in his excitement to bring you to justice, he forgot to take your cash! You come down, you can buy the girl back! Maybe." Laughter. "Don't take long! I don't know how long we can hold off the hounddogs!

Surely not much longer than sunup!" There was more laughter, then Pluto disappeared beneath the awning of the boardwalk.

It was true, Ki thought, the sheriff had neglected to strip his prisoner of his money. But Ki wasn't in any bargaining mood. He moved back to Stone, who was now standing.

"Stone, why did they beat you up?"

"Because I'm a bounty hunter."

Ki nodded. "You protected Jessie, didn't you?"

"I would've died protecting her, Ki. That's some woman, a good woman. I'd hate like hell for anything to happen to her. What was that asshole barking up here about?"

"They're holding Christine as a hostage. More like a piece of meat for the dogs. They want me to come down and buy her back with the money I won in the fight."

Stone chuckled, but there was no mirth to the sound. "So, let's go down and do some business. Some killing business."

Ki looked at the sky. "It'll be dawn in about two hours."

"You think there's really any time to waste?"

"We won't be wasting time. Give them down there time to sweat it out, maybe get a little drunker. Then we go in."

They waited until the first dirty gray light of dawn broke across the sky.

Stone, gunbelt on, guided his mount around the north edge of town. Ki waited until he was in place. Stone had had an extra revolver in his saddlebag, a .44 Colt, which he'd given Ki and which Ki now wore tucked inside his sash.

His hand draped over the hilt of his *katana*, Ki slowly began descending the rise. Ki was in a killing mood.

Chapter 9

A funereal silence hung over Haley. It was a silence so heavy Ki could hear the creak of horse leather and the light clop of hooves as Stone slowly rode his mount around the corner of the buildings at the east edge of town. A deathly silence so thick—where not even a drunken laugh or whoop of lust-fueled delight broke through the batwings of the Comet— that Ki could hear the buzzing of flies close by. East of Haley, the first soft rays of dawn broke across the sky, skeletal pink fingers clawing over the jagged black ridges in the distant desert.

Fisting the hilt of his *katana*, Ki walked into town, as a hot wind lashed dust and grit around the half-Japanese, half-American warrior and sent a piece of tumbleweed skittering behind him. Other than a dozen or so mounts, hitched to railings on both sides of the street, there were no visible signs of life. A horse whickered. Passing the first buildings, Ki spotted his black gelding and the mount Christine had ridden into Haley on. Nothing much stirred but dust. If he hadn't known better, Ki would've sworn Haley was deserted, a ghost town where only the ghosts of the dead and damned now dwelled. Soon, he knew, all that would be left of Haley *would be* the dead and the damned. As Stone had said before they'd split up, they were going to make the Devil dance to their tune.

Haley was about to become Helltown.

For Ki had two immediate goals. One objective was to haul Christine, safe, unharmed, and unsoiled from the clutches of the pimp. And the second was to take no prisoners while putting the torch to the town. Ki and Stone knew what had to be done, and their bond, their contract, was about to be sealed in blood and slaughter.

In the distance through the gloomy shadows, Ki, eyelids slitted to mere cracks, keeping hard vigilance on the boardwalks and the curtains of the boarding rooms, glimpsed Stone as the bounty hunter dismounted in front of the Hotel Haley. There, Stone hitched his mount to the railing and unsheathed his Winchester rifle. The rifle canted to its shoulder, the broad shadow of the bounty hunter glided away from the hotel. Suddenly jacking the lever action on his rifle, a sound of metal on metal that knifed the ghostly silence, Stone walked down the middle of the street, slow, grim, his battered face outlined in a soft yellow glow from the lanterns hung and still burning from the boardwalk awnings.

Flies buzzed.

Boots crunched over stone.

A door creaked open.

Tumbleweed rolled behind Ki.

A horse whinnied.

Right away, Ki recognized the portly figure of Sheriff Doughty and the tall, skinny shadow of his deputy as they eased through the door of their office and stepped out into the street.

"We ain't part of the pimp's deal, mister," Doughty growled into the oppressive silence. "Now . . . you can come peacefully, or you can go feet-first . . . to the undertaker. What'll it be?"

"Some deal you offer. Kindly suggest you butt out, Sheriff," Ki told Doughty, digging a *shuriken* out of his vest, already knowing how the lawman would respond. "Or for you, it's going to be the end."

"Why, you smart-mouth shit . . ."

Predictably, the sheriff draped a hand over his revolver. He drew iron, but Ki had already sent the *shuriken* whirling through the air, a silver blur knifing through soft lamplight. A heartbeat later, Doughty was screaming, hitting his knees, clawing at the steel star impaled in his forearm.

With long, swift strides, Ki moved toward the sheriff.

"You bastard!" Doughty roared. "You can't assault a peace officer!"

Deputy Marlin drew his revolver. A shot rang out, and the Colt was flying from the deputy's hand. Marlin crumpled to a knee beside the wailing sheriff, blood streaming off his hand.

A rifle lever jacked a shell into place. Ki twisted his head a little and saw Stone still slowly advancing down the street.

"You're welcome, Ki," he called out in a quiet voice.

Angling toward the lawmen, Ki touched the brim of his Stetson in silent gratitude to the bounty hunter. Then, like a hurricane, he blew over the dirty law of Haley. Doughty's face was a twisted mask of rage and agony, as he kept cursing Ki. Ki abruptly silenced the sheriff with a jaw-breaking snapkick. The blow lifted Doughty several inches off his knees and flipped him on his back in a heap of billowing dust. Blood poured from the sheriff's mouth, and flies swarmed in, teeming over the crimson froth spilling from Doughty that was dribbling into the parched soil. Marlin was shocked, then livid with fury, at the sight of the beating. Still he was terrified of Ki, and he hesitated, scrabbling through the dust for his discarded revolver. Ki speared the deputy in the face with his knee. As Marlin's head snapped back and he stumbled up on the planks, Ki cycloned into a reverse spinning kick, pulverizing the deputy's face into shattered bone. Driven by rage and pure adrenaline, as the deputy's cry of agony ripped the silence and Marlin struggled to stay standing, Ki drove the heel of his palm into the deputy's nose. As blood sprayed from the pulped ruins of Marlin's nose, the deputy crashed through the plate-glass window of the jail office. Jagged teeth of huge glass shards rained down as Marlin disappeared in a heap into the shadows beyond the devastated window.

Ki backed out into the street. He saw Stone looking up and sideways, the bounty hunter's eyes piercing pinpoints of savage determination and concentration. Ki glimpsed the rifle muzzle poking past the curtain of the window of a second-story boarding room. He saw that the rifleman was trying to draw a bead on him. But a split second later, Stone's rifle cracked a round and shattered glass in that window, and the rifle and the shadow beyond the curtain vanished. In the echo of the killing shot, Ki caught the heavy thud of dead meat hitting the floor beyond that window. For long moments, several horses, spooked by gunfire and crashing glass, whinnied, threatening to break their reins free from the railing.

Then Ki heard the sounds of boots crunching stone, the soft jingle of spurs behind him. Slowly, his hand falling over the butt of his Colt, he turned.

Kiley, Ollie, Crawford, and another gunman were angling away from the side of a building at the west edge of town. Slowly, the foursome fanned out across the street, advancing.

Winchester in hand, Stone jacked another round into place and loped up beside Ki. Spreading out, Ki and Stone faced the four gunmen.

And four faces of rage and hate stared at Ki and Stone through the murky shadows. Ki felt eyes boring into his side. Out of the corner of his eye, he saw the shadows standing behind the plate-glass window of the Comet. The silence once again became so heavy, Ki would've sworn he could hear the heartbeats of the four gunmen.

Ollie now had his gun holstered for a cross draw, since Ki had rendered one of his arms useless. Beside Ollie, Kiley limped along, one of his bowlegs now a bum leg, a bloody bandage around it from when Ki had speared him earlier with a *shuriken*. And Crawford's face was a swollen lump of black-and-purple flesh from the terrible, quick beating Ki had punished him with upstairs in the Comet. Ki didn't recognize the other gunslick.

"We ain't part of the pimp's deal either, you son of a bitch!" Ollie snarled through a shattered, toothless mouth. "Get ready to suck on the Devil's cock, you shit!"

Kiley's gunhand twitched. "Payback."

A fly buzzed around the sweaty, blood-caked face of Crawford.

Tumbleweed rolled behind the four gunmen.

"Take the two on my left," Stone breathed in a tight voice edged with steel and cold anger. "Two on your right, they're yours."

And the four gunmen snaked hands for revolvers.

Stone's Winchester came hurling down, barrel cupped in his hand, as he triggered a round that cracked through Crawford's forehead and puked out a bloody tuft of skull as it exited the back of his head and sent the gunman's Stetson flying behind a pink mist.

A bolt of steel lightning, Ki's Colt was drawn and spitting out flame and lead.

Stone unleathered his Remington in the blink of an eye, blasting a .44 round that bore into Ollie's heart, spraying tattered cloth and crimson mist over his contorted death mask.

Crawford and Ollie spun, pitched to the street, hell-bound.

Kiley took a round to the gut; then Ki triggered his Colt again and shattered the bowlegged gunman's face with a round that smashed through the bridge of his nose. As Kiley snapped backward, ramrod stiff, Ki's Colt flamed again, blasting open a hole dead center in the last gunman's chest. The gunman triggered a wild round in death throes as he plunged for the dirt, his stray shot ricocheting off the street.

A whining echo of gunshot faded off in the distance.

Dust wafted over the four gunmen, and blood sprinkled down over dead, twitching limbs.

Payback.

Instantly, Ki and Stone hit crouches, fanning the gloom with their weapons, searching the buildings for any sign of ambushers.

There were no more takers.

The tumbleweed rolled out of sight.

The hungry buzzing of feeding flies cut the silence.

Stone looked at Ki, a grim smile on his punished face. "Shall we? You first. It's your show."

"My show? For a supporting act, you aren't doing so bad."

Stone replaced the spent shells in his Remington, then dug into his pocket and handed Ki three .44 rounds for his Colt.

Stone nodded at the Comet. "Well, Ki, shall we enter the ninth circle of Hell?"

With Stone watching his back, Ki moved toward the batwings of the Comet, slipping the fully loaded Colt inside his sash.

"Come on in. Now that you've had your fun, let's talk business."

The pimp's laughing voice cut the silence. As he heard two hands smacking together in slow mock clapping, Ki stepped up on the boardwalk. Then he pushed through the batwings and moved inside, with Stone at his back. And Ki found a dozen gunmen perched and lounging around the bar and gaming tables, several whores with fear in their eyes and strangled gasps in their throats sitting in the deep shadows. And Christine, bound and gagged, her eyes bulging with terror, but looking otherwise unharmed and unsoiled, was flanked by two more gunmen as she sat roped to a chair at the far end of the bar. Madame Cheri, Ki saw, had her fat, perfumed carcass perched on a stool, midway down the bar. She put her ruby red lips on a whiskey bottle, drank, then chuckled.

"Some manners in the beginning might've saved you a lot of trouble, Wiseass," she told Ki, who ignored her and walked straight up to Edwards. "Bastard. You'd better learn some respect for a lady and quick!"

Ki turned sideways and grinned back at Madame Cheri. "I do have some respect for a lady. Trouble is, there's only one in here and she can't speak for herself at the moment."

The pimp chuckled.

Madame Cheri hissed, "Bastard!"

The pimp, puffing on a cigar, was seated at his table near the foot of the stairs. Pluto was standing next to him, a smug look on his face, his massive arms folded across his chest, the ivory-handled butt of a .44 Colt tucked inside his belt. Edwards removed his cigar and took a long swig from a bottle of whiskey, then set it down on the table.

Ki stood right before him, hard-eyed, unmoving.

Stone eased up to the bar, steely-eyed vigilance focused on the gunmen around the room, Winchester canted to his shoulder. Gunmen sitting at or around gaming tables smoked cigars, swilled beer, and sucked down whiskey, eyeing Ki and Stone through narrow gazes.

Edwards clapped. "Bravo. Nicely done. Since the sheriff, his lackey, and the others didn't see fit to

116

indulge me in my deal, well, Ki, you just got rid of some dead weight. Heh-heh, I like that, dead weight, get it? I hear something about sucking the Devil's cock out there?" He peered at Ki, chuckled, shook his head. "My, that's some ugly kinda talk. Downright nasty." He shuddered. "Uh. The image that conjures up, and in the mind of a former preacher, no less. Loose tongues, no respect. I tell ya, what's the world coming to?"

Through a cold slit-eyed gaze, Ki watched Edwards and his muscle. "Where did they take Jessie?"

"Sounds like you expect to leave here alive, boy," Pluto rumbled, unfolding his arms. Ki tensed and prepared to draw as Pluto draped a ham-size fist over his Colt.

"Now, now, Pluto, please," Edwards chided. "No more gunplay, violence isn't what we're about. We're about love; we're about the pleasures of the flesh, not pain. Now," he said to Ki, "by 'they,' I suppose you mean Haley and the others. Well, 'they' had some business to attend to."

"What kind of business? Where?"

"My, my, you are pushy," Edwards laughed. He puffed on his cigar and blew smoke at Ki. "Durango. It's a prison about a half—"

"I know where it is," Stone called out.

"Well, now that we've got that straightened out," Edwards chortled. "Let's talk. You wanna make some easy money, mister?"

"The girl. Hand her over, we'll walk out of here. And you can go on pimping. You hope."

Edwards shook his head. He snapped his fingers. "Stella!" Moments later, a blond whore walked across the room. She sat in the pimp's lap. He squeezed her breasts. "Look at these yams, will ya? Big, juicy, mouth-watering tits. You like them? You wanna suck 'em? I know I wanna suck 'em. Only problem, they ain't firm and young and ripe like your little girlfriend sitting over there, all pretty and sweet-looking, ready for some real fun. I'll even wager her bush smells as sweet as apple pie, young as she is."

The whore scowled at the implied insult, but sat there, a piece of fleshly putty in the pimp's hands as he kept kneading her big, floppy tits.

Ki felt his blood boil. "The girl."

"That's what I'm trying to talk to you about here, hardhead. Hardhead, get it? Don't the sight of these big suckers," Edwards laughed, twisting the whore's tits, "make you want her? Hardhead."

"One more time. The girl."

"Why all this fuss over one little trollop?" Edwards growled. "Surely, we can come to some sort of arrangement, for both you and your friend over there. Lighten up, take the day off, it'll be on me. Any girl you want, all the liquor you can drink."

"You can buy a lot of things, Pimp, but you can't buy honor or respect," Ki said. "And you can't buy me."

"Why not? I could use a good man like you and your friend. I could take this whole town when Haley and the others ride back."

Ki clenched his teeth, feeling his rage rising. "They won't be riding back."

"Oh, you're so noble," Edwards said. "You mean to tell me you're willing to die for that little suck-bitch over there?" Edwards shook his head. "Oh, yes, honor and nobility, virtue. Well, I used to be a preacher once. I even used those words myself a time or two. You believe that, me a preacher, a man of God?"

Ki said nothing.

"It's true. Back in Kansas. Depressing occupation really. Seeing the same people, day in and day out. Dragging their little squalid, squawling, miserable brats along to hear me proclaim the nobility of righteous clean living. Looking out from the pulpit and seeing all those lives of drudgery, I knew they couldn't stand, you know, the common stink of the common man. Too damn scared to live like they want, too damn scared to die, fearing the wrath of God or some such bullshit if their souls aren't right with Jesus. Their dead, listless faces, their yearning voices, empty of life and all desire, content, they think, to wait for something I'm telling 'em is there, you know—their reward in Heaven after death. Bah! Actually, I made a few dollars. Used to skim a nice little haul out of the collection baskets every week. Got bored, though. I guess the narrow path just wasn't meant for me. Oh, well.

"So I set out and ended up here after rounding up a nice little traveling caravan of ladies. Turned the old man—that's Mr. Haley, by the way—turned him on to more than a few nights of my comely trollops. Put our heads together in a nice little business arrangement for his town. Get it? Put our heads together? Heh-heh. Now, Haley pays good, but not good enough. That's where our business comes in, Mr. Ki. I want you and your friend. I want your guns. I want your sword and those feet and fists of bone-breaking hellish fury I seen you unleash on some poor souls. I want your balls; I want your souls. And I want the girl. Now, we can do this nice and peaceful, or I can kill you and your friend right here and now, and take what I want. Hey, I'm trying to be decent about this. Look, it's in your best interest to cooperate here. Hell, just look around. I got women, I got money, I got all the booze a man can drink, I got gambling, I got it all! What more could a man want?"

"That's where you're wrong, Pimp, dead wrong," Ki said. "You see, you don't have a damn thing I want. Except the girl."

Ki looked over his shoulder, met Stone's gaze, nodded. And Ki exploded. With one hand, he pulled his Colt out of the sash, cocked it, and shot Pluto in the face. As Pluto's blood washed over Edwards, Ki scooped up the whiskey bottle and, in one lightning motion, smashed the bottle in the pimp's face.

With grim determination, Stone triggered his Winchester and fired a bullet through the heart of one of the gunmen flanking Christine. All hell broke loose.

Chapter 10

As the pimp toppled out of his chair, clutching his bloody face and wailing, "My eyes, my eyes!" at the top of his lungs and the blond whore pitched sideways out of Edwards's lap and shrieked in terror, Ki became a whirlwind of terrible violence that ripped through the Comet.

Of course, he got by with a little help from his bounty hunter friend.

Stone was triggering one round after another from his smoking, flaming Winchester, scattering outlaws under a sizzling hail of lead, exploding glasses and bottles in their faces, drenching them in blood, beer, and sweat. Having jacked the rifle's action twice more, drilling two outlaws around the gaming tables in the chest and kicking them back behind crimson mists and tattered cloth, Stone rolled over the bar top as slugs began peppering wood and shattering glass around him.

Madame Cheri cursed and belly flopped to the

floor as liquor bottles exploded behind her, gunmen spraying the bar front with wild fire from bucking revolvers. Beneath the umbrella of soft yellow light burning from kerosene lanterns hung from the ceiling, she looked like a big, redheaded slug, rolls of fat quivering in sheer fright. "You crazy bastards, don't shoot me!" she roared, as her beehive hairdo was parted down the middle by a bullet, scissored strands of hair flying above her.

Pivoting, crouched, Ki sent a *shuriken* twirling across the room, the steel star spinning past Christine's horrified stare and cracking into the temple of the other gunman beside her. That gunman twitched and jerked, triggering a round into the ceiling as he danced in death throes then tumbled into a row of liquor bottles. Colt in hand in the next heartbeat, Ki turned the face of the nearest outlaw, blowing him into bloody mush with one thundering round.

Stone popped up over the bar front, triggered his Winchester, and fired a slug into the side of another gunman's head, hurling him back and crashing down through a gaming table, turning wood into matchsticks as whores nose-dived to the floor, out of the crossfire. In three long strides, crouched beneath the bar top, as bottles and the mirror that ran the length of the bar exploded in a tidal wave of razoring glass, Stone reached Christine. With one strong swoop of his arm, he hooked the back of her chair in a clawed hand and pulled her behind the bar as bullets whined off the floor around her. Another bullet sizzled from the bounty hunter's rifle, and he kicked a gunman through the plate-glass window, flinging him to the planks beyond beneath a shower of glass shards.

"My eyes! Oh, God, oh, God! Am I blind?"

Ki threw the pimp's table up in the air, a split second before slugs tattooed the table, hurling wood slivers into his face. Glancing sideways, Ki saw the pimp staring at his blood-soaked hands. Glass bits were impaled in his face, just below his eyes. No, the pimp wasn't blind, but being blind became the least of his troubles in the next heartbeat.

Suddenly realizing there was only the bitter sting of blood in his eyes and not glass, Edwards found the strength and the courage of the mad. His bloody mask twisted with rage and hate, he grabbed the Colt off Pluto's body. "You bastard! You could've blinded me!"

Ki kicked the gun out of Edwards's hand and sent it spinning away. Then Edwards leapt to his feet, hands like the claws of a buzzard as he lunged at Ki. It proved a fatal move for the pimp.

As a chunk of wood was sheared off by gunfire and sliced past his face, Ki, out of the corner of his eye, saw three outlaws charging his way. As their revolvers flamed, he grabbed Edwards and spun him around, right into the line of fire from the kill-crazed outlaws.

With three lightning rounds from his Winchester, Stone opened the stomach and chest of an outlaw, kicking him, backpedaling, through a shard of hanging glass and out of the Comet. Stone kept jacking the lever action, picking off more outlaws with lethal marksmanship.

Blood-soaked bodies danced and toppled all over the room, under the bounty hunter's flaming lead death. Whores shrieked as they crawled for cover beneath the gaming tables.

Bullets marched up and down the pimp's suit jacket. Edwards screamed, as Ki held him upright, using the pimp as a shield, firing around his convulsing body, gouging open the chest of one outlaw with two quick rounds. As the pimp's red suit jacket was turned into tattered crimson shreds and a slug whizzed past Ki's ear, the half-Japanese, half-American warrior picked Edwards up off his feet. Fueled by rage, fear, and adrenaline, Ki found sudden Herculean reserves of strength and hurled the body of Edwards into the two outlaws bulling his way. Behind the plummeting weight of the pimp, the outlaws crashed to the floor. Colt blazing, Ki ripped open the chest of an outlaw darting for cover behind the splintered halves of a gaming table. As he spun and pitched into beds of broken glass, Ki unsheathed his sword. And as one outlaw rolled the body of Edwards off him, Ki shot the other gunman in the face with his last round.

Stone took down another outlaw target with Winchester lead, cracking open his skull, midway across the room, hammering him on top of a whore seeking shelter.

The last surviving outlaw bolted to his feet. His gun was tracking around for a shot at Ki, but Ki speared him through the stomach. The tip of the samurai sword burst out of the gunman's back. Ki held him upright for an eternal second, staring right into the outlaw's bulging eyes as blood sprayed from his back. Then Ki slowly slid the sword free, the outlaw crumpling at his feet. He wiped the blade clean on the back of the gunman's twitching legs and sheathed the sword.

An outlaw, slumped in death over an upturned table, twitched once, then slid down the table and thudded to the floor, trailing a greasy smear of red on the green table felt.

Ki, heart pounding in his ears, adrenaline still racing through him, looked at Christine, as Stone took a knife from behind the bar and cut her free.

"You crazy . . . You crazy asshole!"

Startled, Ki wheeled, and spotted the tiny derringer in Madame Cheri's fat hand. The derringer cracked, but Ki was already darting sideways as the slug drilled into a table beside him. Madame Cheri tried to stand, but she wobbled, then slipped on some spilled liquor, her boots crunching glass. Ki was all over her within three swift strides as she caught her balance and stayed standing. He wrenched the derringer out of her hand, eyes blazing with cold fury. Ki looked at the pocket pistol. It was a Philadelphia Derringer .41, the original 1825 model invented by Henry Derringer, a small backup piece that could be used by even the toughest of gunfighters. But the madam wasn't any gunfighter in Ki's eyes; she was just plain ugly, in every sense. He tossed the derringer aside.

"You're dead. You'll never leave this town alive," Madame Cheri snarled, and spat in Ki's face. "Not when Mr. Haley and the others get back."

With the back of his hand, Ki wiped the spit off his face. "I never hit women," he said through clenched teeth. "Or, rather, I should say I never hit ladies. Your case is different, and I make a proud exception."

With just enough force to make her face sting, Ki backhanded the madam square in the mouth, slamming her back into the bar.

"Ki!"

125

Ki reached Christine, took her by the shoulders, and hugged her. "Are you all right?"

"Y-yes, I'm all right. They said you didn't have the guts to come here . . . You should've heard the terrible things they were saying about you."

Christine kissed Ki on the mouth. Her lips tasted as sweet, as fiery, as ever to Ki. He pulled back. He was glad she was unhurt.

"Christine, we have to go," Ki told her. "Listen to me. From here on, you do exactly as I say, when I say, if you want to stay alive. You understand? I thank you for breaking me out of jail, but no more wild stunts like that, okay?"

Christine nodded that she understood.

"Stone, you know what we have to do."

"I suggest," the bounty hunter called out across the room, "that everybody clear this place out in the next few minutes."

"Wh-what are you going to do?" Madame Cheri asked.

Ki cocked a grin over his shoulder at the madam, as he led Christine toward the batwings. "We're going to warm that cold heart of yours up a little, Madame. The Comet's about to flame out, you might say."

Striking a match off the bar top, Stone lit a kerosene lamp. "Madame, is there anybody upstairs?"

Madame Cheri's lip quivered, as realization filled her eyes with terror. "Why . . . Oh, God." She turned and waddled toward the stairs. She hollered up the steps. Seconds later, as Stone pitched the lamp to the floor, glass shattering and flames licking away at dry wood, a long line of whores descended the steps in various states of disarray and undress, followed by a few johns who'd wisely chosen to sit out the barroom fight to the death.

Quickly, Stone reloaded his Winchester, then began shooting out the ceiling lamps. Tongues of fiery kerosene and twinkling glass slivers rained down on the room. Rifle in hand, Stone hit the street, whores and their johns scrambling out of the Comet behind him.

Ki led Christine to her horse and helped her into the saddle as she slipped her feet into the stirrups. From the saddlebag of his gelding, Ki took his Colt. Shadows of men and women were now moving out into the street from all buildings.

"Ahhh! You're . . . under arrest, m-m-mister!"

Wheeling, Ki found Sheriff Doughty wobbling to his feet. The sheriff cried out in pain as he stood, blood still soaking into his shirtfront, as he grimaced, touching his swollen jaw. It must've taken a whole lot of strength, Ki figured, for the sheriff to get those words out through his shattered mouth.

Obviously not having learned his lesson, Doughty was reaching for his discarded revolver.

Ki sent a *shuriken* spinning the sheriff's way. And then fresh waves of agony ripped across Doughty's face as the steel star tore into the back of his hand. Doughty screamed, stood ramrod stiff for a second, and then toppled, fainting from the pain.

As whores and johns kept rushing out of the Comet, flames leaping across the gaming room, Stone began shooting out the lanterns up and down the street with his Winchester. Townspeople cursed and shouted, but no one moved to stop Ki or Stone. Horses whinnied in panic, some snapping their reins free from railings as smoke billowed out of the Comet and began eating up the planks on both sides of the street.

Christine eased her mount out into the middle of the street, her eyes wide with a mix of fear and awe as she stared at the flames eating away the insides of the Comet.

Ki, sword in hand, cut free the horses that hadn't snapped their reins loose. He mounted his gelding.

With the barrel of his rifle, Stone unhooked a lantern as he strode for the Hotel Haley.

Grim-faced, revolver in hand, watching their backs, Ki led Christine to the east end of town. There, Stone hurled a lantern through the plate-glass window of the hotel.

Cursing and shouting hit Ki's back as he rode past Stone and up the east rise.

Haley burned, and Ki only wished he could see the look on the face of the man who had built this town when he saw the whole damn place going up in flames.

But Max Haley wasn't coming back here, not if Ki could help it. If anyone harmed one hair on Jessie's head, Ki thought, that man would die. Slowly and in great pain.

The sun cleared the east hills, a fiery orange eye ready to burn the desert and turn it once again into a cruel wasteland.

Ki, Stone, and Christine were several miles across the broken plateau, riding at an easy canter away from the hellstorm raging behind them. Cactus, scrub brush, and rock reached for as far as the eye could see. Ki slowed his mount as he saw Stone nearly topple from the saddle. Ki reined his gelding in, and Christine rode her horse to a stop beside him.

Stone spat blood, and his eyes glazed over for a moment as he sat still in the saddle.

"Stone? Are you all right?" Ki asked.

Stone nodded. "Yeah. I'll be okay." He sucked in a deep breath. "I don't have time to hurt, not where we're going and what we're up against."

Ki took a moment to look behind him. West, huge billowing black clouds of smoke smudged the blue sky, marking the funeral pyre of Haley. Ki made out the black, winged shapes of buzzards circling the smoke clouds. There would be plenty of cold, dead flesh back there for the scavenger birds to feast on, Ki knew.

"Stone," Ki said, "what is this prison, Durango? I've never heard of it."

"It's where they send the worst of the worst."

"Why would Haley go there with his pack?"

Stone shrugged. He took a deep swallow from his canteen and seemed steadier as a few seconds of silence passed and he soaked it up.

"Good question, Ki. Only one way to find out. And you know, my friend, as ugly as things were back there, they'll be a whole helluva lot uglier when we catch up to Haley and Brutus. We've got a good half day's ride ahead of us to Durango. Shall we?"

Ki looked at Christine, concerned for her safety. "Stay real close to me, Christine. If I see trouble ahead, I'm going to have to hide you away someplace."

She looked set to protest, but Ki injected steel into his eyes.

Stone was right, and Ki could tell Christine knew it.

Whatever lay ahead, Ki knew it was going to be far worse than the orgy of death they had left behind in Haley.

Chapter 11

The pounding of hooves thundered over the edge of the hill. The sun blazed a hellish fury from a blue sky of high noon.

A wall of billowing dust surged over the lip of the rise, and seconds later Max Haley, Brutus, and his outlaw pack reined in their mounts along the edge.

Jessie sat in the saddle of her mount, up front and next to Haley. She wore a brown Stetson Haley had earlier ordered one of Brutus's guns to give to her, to shield her face from the savage pounding of the sun. And the only hatless rider in the bunch was Hanks, who hadn't said the first word in protest or even given the slightest hint of a scowl when commanded to turn his hat over to Jessie. It was so hot now the air felt to Jessie as if it burned her throat. And her clothes were drenched in sweat, caked with grit. Haley had earlier chuckled that he wished he'd brought along a change of decent clothes for her, but being uncomfortable in the saddle was the least of her worries. What Jessie wanted most was her weapons, but Brutus was holding onto her Colt and derringer, and it didn't look as if she'd be getting her guns back anytime soon. No, what she wanted most of all right then was for Ki and Stone to show up, so that she would know they were safe.

So that the three of them could tear this pack of wolves apart.

Grim silence hovered over the outlaw pack and the beautiful heiress, horses whickering, their flanks wet with lather from what Jessie guessed had been a hard six maybe seven hours' ride across the desert. The way these men pushed their horses, she'd seen, it was obvious they gave their mounts about as much consideration as they did human life. None.

And she was still just Jessie to Max Haley. And it would remain that way. Since the Starbuck name was famous, as was the Lone Star legend, Jessie could ill afford to reveal who she really was to Haley.

Dust swirling around his face, Haley peered down into the valley with a look of morbid fascination. "Welcome to Durango, Jessie. Some might say welcome to Hell."

One of the outlaws behind Jessie chuckled, "But most call this place the Devil's Asshole."

Haley glared over his shoulder at the gunman. "Watch your filthy mouth. You understand me, mister?"

"Yeah, I gotcha," the offending outlaw grumbled.

Indeed, the prison called Durango looked ominous, fearsome, to Jessie. Below them, in a valley ringed by jagged ridges that looked like the teeth of some carnivore, the prison appeared to have been built, or rather dug, down into the bowels of the earth. It was the literal blackness of the prison that struck Jessie and sent a chill down her spine. The front wall appeared to run about three hundred feet across to Jessie, and the front gate was open, a big maw right in the middle of the wall. Those walls rose, she judged, about twenty feet in the air. Against the far south wall, she saw a long, two-story block structure, stretching from the east to the west wall. There were iron-barred windows set in that black-painted structure, dozens of them, spaced about ten feet apart. In the courtyard, she saw guards milling around two smaller buildings, near an iron-barred wagon used to haul prisoners. There was a gallows in the middle of the courtyard and two small, black box-shaped objects near the hangman's stage. Other similar boxlike structures were planted near the base of the west wall. There was only one guard tower, a timber box-shaped black structure that loomed ten feet higher than the front wall. A guard was in that tower, looking their way, a rifle in his hands.

"I know the color kind of catches you off-guard at first," Haley explained. "Walls are corrugated iron, and they painted them black, but for a reason. Draws the sun, see. Just like hellfire inside. Finished building this place about six months ago, so its reputation really hasn't spread real far and wide yet. Most men sent here to do time . . . well, many will probably end up doing eternity, I understand. That's the general idea, though. When they ride up, chained down like animals in a wagon, see the color, feel the heat, smell the stink of the damned, see a few buzzards circling the walls above, they know they've surely reached the end of the line. They find themselves staring right into the gates of Hell.

"I was told a lot of horses died hauling those sections of iron across the desert. Understand a lot of men died, too, in the heat from putting them up. And guess who built it? That's right. The prisoners, or the condemned, I should say. They were made to build their own little corner of Hell here in the desert. Now the warden, Bob Teetleman, he's a good friend of mine. I've sent Big John here a couple of times to do some recruiting. But that's not why we're here."

Jessie asked, "Then why are we here?"

Haley chuckled. "To pick up a quarter-million stash in gold ingots. You see, sometime tomorrow morning, the governor of this Territory, a few politicians from back east, and about a dozen federal marshals are riding in. I want to buy me a state, Jessie, and the suits from back east are going to help me push statehood through in Washington. Plus, with some marshals in my pocket, well, hell, Jessie, who's gonna stop me? From there, I might even buy up the Army. But I'll work on that angle in due time. The deal here, it's all been prearranged. I just have to pay those men and they belong to me. That's why we're meeting here, on my turf, on my terms. Out of the way, damn near out of the reach of all civilization, if it weren't for my town. Still think I'm a man dreaming the impossible dream?"

No, the man wasn't any dreamer, Jessie decided. Haley was insane. But he had the clout, both in guns and gold, to maybe pull it off. Unless she did something. But what? And how? *Where are you, Ki? Where are you, Stone?* And she took a moment to wonder about Christine, hoping the girl was safe and unharmed.

"Why are you here, Jessie?" Haley went on. "Well, I thought out of the kindness of my heart, I'd give you a second chance to reconsider my earlier proposition."

Jessie said nothing, but she wished she had her guns back to do her talking for her.

Haley shrugged. "Still no answer? Well, you've got a while yet. The way you're looking at me, Jessie, I can almost hear you thinking, He's crazy. Maybe I am. Maybe we all are—for even being out here in this heat, that is, instead of someplace right cozy, with a brandy snifter in hand. You know, I often thought it was a shame I never married, never had any children to carry on the Haley line. But, who knows, Jessie, who knows what's in the cards? Maybe I'll have that child yet. I'd like a boy. I'd like to see the Haley line live on. A man without any children, well, unless he's built something, created something, his life can feel mighty empty." Haley narrowed his gaze, staring at Jessie, hard-eyed. "The time we're here, Jessie, I want you to think hard, real hard, about what you want. It could be a matter of life and death."

"That's all I've been thinking about, life and death," Jessie told Haley, then looked past him, at Brutus. For a second, she would have sworn she detected something flicker through his eyes, some hint of a scheme. The big outlaw seemed harder to her, more deadly than ever. Something didn't feel right to her. There was something in Brutus's silence—no, she felt it in the silence and saw it in the eyes of all his outlaws, too.

"Let's ride, boys," Haley commanded, and urged his mount ahead and down into the valley. "It's payday, just like I promised you."

As they reached level ground and rode for the opening, Jessie spotted a lone buzzard spreading its wings and wheeling for the sky.

"Max Haley to see the warden!" Haley called up to the guard tower.

"Hey!" the guard bellowed down into the courtyard. "Get the warden! Mr. Haley's here!"

As they rode through the gate opening and into the sprawling courtyard, a vile stench assaulted Jessie's senses. What she smelled, she knew, was the stink of sweat, and human suffering. The stink of things dying. The stink of despair.

The smell of fear and death.

And the stifling heat made Jessie feel as if she'd just ridden into a furnace. It was hotter inside those black walls than she could have ever imagined. Hot as hellfire.

Above the prison, a lone buzzard floated in the blue sea of the burning sky.

Jessie took in her surroundings, following Haley toward what she guessed were the warden's quarters. About a dozen horses were hitched to a railing beside those quarters, drinking from a water trough and eating from feed bags. There was a stack of loose lumber beside the hitching rail, some rope and hammers. Durango, Jessie suspected, was still in the process of construction, or maybe they were going to be building another gallows. She wondered how many men had died here. Haley was right. If ever there was such a thing as hell on earth, this prison was it.

Seconds later, the door opened to those quarters near the horses. A tall man dressed in black, from Stetson to suit jacket to boots, strode away from the building. Haley proved Jessie's guess right about that building as he said, "Warden, good to see you again."

"Good to see you, too, Max."

As Haley reined his mount in before the warden, Jessie took a harder look at the man who ran Durango. She was struck by how skinny he was. He looked like a scarecrow; the flesh on his gaunt, clean-shaven face was stretched taut over high cheekbones. He looked white as a ghost to Jessie.

"How's the town?"

Haley smiled at the warden as Teetleman stopped in front of the outlaw pack. "She's still standing. And she's still expanding. She's my baby, Bob, guess you might compare her to a woman who's now about two months pregnant."

The warden noticed Jessie, a scowl twisting one side of his pale face. "Who's your lady friend, Max?"

"This is Jessie," Haley said. "And, yeah, she's a friend of mine, a real special friend. Want her treated with the utmost dignity and respect."

Jessie said nothing.

Teetleman peered at Jessie. "Pardon me for being a little presumptuous, Max, but she don't look all too happy being here."

Haley chuckled. "Hell, can you blame her? Ah, she's along for the ride, Bob. Might say I'm trying to make an impression on the lady."

"So, take her to New York City or San Francisco."

"Some other time, Bob, some other time."

"Jesus, boys, look at this! A woman!"

All heads turned sideways. Jessie followed the eyes of the outlaws and the warden toward the cell blocks. There, she saw the shadowy faces of dozens of bearded, sweaty men pressed up against iron-barred windows. Whistling and catcalling bellowed across the courtyard.

"Man-o-man, thanks, Warden, I knew you had a heart inside that old bag a bones! You dirty ol' bastard, you, now bring on the rest of the whores! We all heard about Haley!"

"C'mon, Teetleman, bring her in here, let me have a go at that sweet stuff!"

"Yeah, Warden, I'm tired of screwing my cellmate! Fact, send someone in here. He ain't movin', I think he's dead; I think I screwed 'im to death! He's startin' to stink!"

Laughter ripped from behind those bars.

"Gawddamn, my eyes deceive me. Is it this goddam heat? Tell me it's true. Tell me that's a woman!"

"It's a woman, awright, Sawyer, and I feel a mean load buildin' up just lookin' at it!"

"Shut up, you men!" Teetleman roared, taking a step away from Haley, toward the cell block.

"Screw you, Warden! What are you gonna do, kill us? C'mon, bring in yer guards. Screw you! I'll kill you, I'll kill you all! I'll screw you so far up yer skinny ass, you'll spit shit! I got nothin' to lose. I got me a date with the hangman day after tomorra, so I'm givin' ya my last request now, you skinny cocksuckin' shit! Send in the bitch!"

"Shut your filthy holes!" Teetleman bellowed. "Next man opens his mouth, I'll have him tossed in a hot box! There's plenty of hellboxes out here. I'll cram every last one of your filthy carcasses in one and leave you there."

The prisoners quieted down. Five guards with Winchesters roamed the front of the cell block, daring anyone to utter another catcall.

And Jessie's gaze followed the warden, as he stood beside one of the hot boxes. Teetleman smiled, patting the top of the squat black box as a father would stroke the head of his child. Jessie noted the small hole in the door of that box, big enough to let in just enough air to keep a man breathing. She caught a faint whiff of feces and urine coming from the boxes and saw a black cloud of flies swirling around them. She shuddered to think of how many prisoners had suffered in one of those hellboxes, wallowing, sweating in their own filth, possibly driven mad by the merciless, unending buzzing of flies. It struck her that here the jailers were no better than the jailed.

"Foul-mouthed vermin," Teetleman grumbled, striding back toward Haley. "I'm sorry, Max. My apologies for that outburst, ma'am."

"Quite okay, Bob. But it looks like you'll have to put me and Jessie up in your quarters for the night."

"Be fine. Got plenty of whiskey in there, even a good bottle of brandy for you. The grub ain't much, can't very well keep steak in this heat, but there's plenty of liquor."

Haley smiled. "Sounds almost like a night in heaven, Bob. Now. Let's take a look at my money. Boys, let's hitch these mounts," Haley told Brutus and his gang. "Stretch your legs. We got all night. Jessie, stick close to me."

Jessie dismounted at the hitching rail along with the other outlaws. She felt tension from the outlaws. No one would look at her; she couldn't even catch Brutus's eye. As Haley took her by the arm, she saw Brutus nod at his men. Some kind of signal? Moments later, she saw outlaws slide rifles from sheaths.

Haley was all smiles as he pulled a set of keys out of his pants pocket, long, swift strides carrying him toward the iron-barred prisoner-transport wagon.

"Ah, Bob," Haley chuckled. "It's payday. And tomorrow, my friend, well, let's just say big things are ahead of us."

Jessie stood behind Haley. She heard keys rattling and glanced at Haley as he opened the padlock, then swung back the heavy iron door to reveal four large metal trunks. All four trunks were locked. Haley opened the trunk closest to him. And countless gold ingots glittered in the fierce sunlight.

"I don't have to count it, do I, Bob?"

Haley was grinning at the warden, but there was ice in his eyes.

Teetleman chuckled and tried to appear nonchalant, but a flicker of anger went through his eyes. "No way was I about to mess up our deal, Max. Not when you promised me ten percent of that gold."

"Wasn't you I was worried about, Bob."

"Well, I haven't left the grounds in six months."

"Bet you haven't even strayed beyond the front gate, right?"

"Right. I made damn sure this wagon was kept under twenty-four-hour guard, just like you asked, Max."

"You're a good man, Bob."

"You're a dead man, Bob."

Haley wheeled, startled.

Jessie turned sideways and found herself staring right into the muzzle of Brutus's Colt.

"What the . . ."

Haley never finished his sentence.

Outlaw rifles began flaming out lead messages of death. Bullets chewed up the wood around the guard in his tower; then a dozen or more slugs peppered him, slicing away chunks of cloth behind crimson sprays. The guard never got off a shot, as he danced around in his tower like a puppet on a string, then crashed through his parapet. Even as he plunged for the courtyard, outlaws, as if it were some game to them, kept drilling his falling body with lead, whooping and hollering in sick delight. There was a horrible crunch of bone as the guard's body hammered to the courtyard, exploding a cloud of dust into the air above his convulsing, bullet-riddled corpse.

But the din of deadly gunfire kept roaring as outlaws advanced on the guards in front of the cell block.

"What the hell is going on here!?" Haley bellowed.

John Brutus just grinned at Max Haley. "What do you think's going on, Max? Sometimes, y'know, you can be so goddam stupid!"

★

Chapter 12

Time felt as if it had frozen for Jessie. As badly off as she was in the lust-seething clutches of Haley, she knew she'd be far worse off when the dust of Brutus's violent takeover settled.

Haley took a step toward the big outlaw. "Brutus, I order you—"

Brutus cocked the hammer on his Colt. "You ain't givin' the orders no more, Max!" he shouted over the relentless cracking of rifles. "One more step, I'll shoot you where you stand!"

Jessie could only watch the slaughter as outlaws swung rifles and revolvers her way.

One guard was pinned to the front of the cell-block wall by a salvo of bullets. The front of his shirt was ripped open by lead, blood spraying over the black walls in thick, greasy smears of crimson. That guard was dead on his feet, but outlaws kept pumping lead into him, even as he slid down the wall in a crumpled heap. A long arm snaked out between the iron bars and wrapped around the neck of another guard.

"I got one! Do 'im! Make the son of a bitch dance!" the prisoner shouted in glee.

And countless slugs tore open that helpless guard, as the prisoner holding him in a deathlock laughed and whooped, the guard jerking and screaming in his arms.

"Don't kill 'em all!" Brutus shouted. "Hold your fire, goddammit! I want some hostages!"

"Drop those guns!" an outlaw ordered the guards near the horses, all of whom seemed paralyzed by shock and fear, as Brutus's cutthroats swarmed over them, stripping them of weapons, then beating them to the ground with fists and rifle butts.

For long moments, the killing shots echoed around the courtyard and horses whinnied in panic.

Out of nowhere, four buzzards appeared, slowly falling from the sky to perch themselves on the walls of Durango.

Brutus strode right up to Haley and snatched the keys out of his hands. "I'll take the keys, Max. I'll take the woman. I'll take the gold. I believe I got it all now. Thank you kindly."

Haley seethed with rage, his whole body trembling, his eyes burning. "Why? I pay you and your men well, now you do this to me!"

Brutus laughed, then punched Haley right in the mouth and dropped him on his back. "There's a lot of whys, Max. The biggest reason I can think of is about a quarter million whys here in gold." Brutus loomed over Haley and kicked him in the ribs, then dug a derringer out of Haley's jacket pocket. "You won't be needing this anymore, Max."

"You'll never get away with this!" Teetleman sputtered.

"I've already gotten away with it," Brutus told the warden.

"What are you going to do?" Teetleman asked.

"Why, I'm going to have some fun for a little while. You don't mind, do you? Good."

"Hey, Big John. You're beautiful, Big Guy. How 'bout sending some of your boys in here and letting us out?" a prisoner hollered.

An excited uproar burst from the cell block.

"Get me outta here, Brutus, now! Get your ass in here!"

"Watch 'em," Brutus ordered his guns, as guards were rounded up and surrounded by outlaws. "Sounds like somebody needs a lesson in respect to me!"

A prisoner kept shouting and demanding Brutus set him free. Jessie saw a face twisted with maniacal rage, straining against the bars of a cell window. What happened next sent a chill down her spine and told her Brutus was more insane than a hundred Max Haleys.

Brutus walked right up to the window of the prisoner screaming for his release and shot that man in the face. Curses and gasps of horror and outrage ripped from the mouths of other prisoners.

"Shut up!" Brutus shouted. "Shut the hell up!"

"You let us outta here, goddammit!"

"Peters, Dretchen, Murphy!" Brutus roared across the courtyard. "Go inside and show these men I want some respect! I want order! I want quiet!"

Jessie watched as Haley picked himself up off the ground. Three outlaws marched toward the cell block, jacking the lever actions on their Winchester rifles. Moments later, they disappeared through the doorway of the cell block, as Brutus, his eyes glowing with an insane lust for power, strode back to the transport wagon. Rifle fire rang out, echoing through the open door of the cell block. Men screamed in agony, shouted curses. Jessie flinched once at the initial volley of weapons fire, then just softly shook her head to herself.

"You're insane," Teetleman told Brutus, his skeletal face etched in horror.

Brutus ran his hands over the gold, his eyes wide. He slammed shut the lid on the trunk, locked it, and pocketed the keys. "No, I'm rich," the big outlaw growled, then grabbed the warden by the shoulder.

"What are you doing to me?" Teetleman gasped. "Where are you taking me?"

"Stop your whining! Just gonna give you some time to cool off, Warden, that's all, so relax," Brutus laughed. He opened the door to the hot box near the gallows.

"No!" Teetleman screamed, as Brutus shoved him into the box, slammed the door, and locked it.

"Have a nice day, Warden," Brutus said, patting the top of the hellbox. "Dig out those sticks! Get the keys off those guards! Find some kerosene and put those guards in the other boxes!"

As the others scrambled to comply with Brutus's orders, the big outlaw marched back to Haley.

"Listen, John," Haley pleaded, "I've got money, more money than that gold you see there. Five, six times as much! We can work something out."

Brutus just shook his head, grinning. "You don't get it, do you, Max?"

"What? Get what? What do you want?"

"I've got what I want right there in that dead man's wagon. And what you don't get is that you, Mr. eh, Big, as I believe the lady here called you earlier, well, Mr. Big, this is about cutting you down to size, the size of a snake, the size of the worm that you really are. You're gonna watch me work this evening. I'm going to put the fear of the Devil in you. Until your little party arrives here tomorrow you're going to know what the fear of death is all about."

"You're going to ambush the governor of this Territory?" Haley asked in cold disbelief. "You're going to bushwack those marshals? Those politicians?"

"You got it. I'm going to leave behind a nice little message for anybody who gets any ideas about following me. You see, Max, me and the boys, we've earned a nice long vacation, south of the border. And anybody who's foolish enough to come into Mexico after us, well, I'll have bought me my own army, the Federales. Some gringo gold will go a long ways down there."

"You're insane," Haley growled.

"I keep hearing that. It's upsetting me." Brutus roared with laughter. "How's it feel, Max? For so long, you thought you were on top of the heap. I let you slap my men around, humiliate them, order them around like greenhorns. Well, it's payday all right, Max. No, it's payback day."

Jessie watched as Brutus wheeled and went up to an outlaw, told him something. She saw sticks of twined dynamite pulled from saddlebags. Guards were ushered toward the other hot boxes. The air was thick with the buzzing of hungry flies. Warden Teetleman's muffled voice of agony cut across the courtyard, as he pounded on the door of the hot box.

Two outlaws walked up to Jessie and Haley. "Big man says to throw you two in jail. Together."

"Cheer up," Brutus called to Jessie and Haley from the gallows. "The party's only begun."

They tossed Jessie and Haley together into a cell of dead men. The stench of blood and death filled Jessie's nose as she stared at two prisoners in her cell who had been shot dead like rats in a barrel. Flies buzzed over the lifeless, blood-streaked faces of the prisoners, who looked up at the ceiling with wide, empty stares.

"Good God, what's to become of me?"

Jessie looked at Haley. He looked shriveled and shrunken, shoulders stooped in despair as he sat on a cot in the far corner of the cell. There, he buried his face in his hands. He looked to Jessie as if he'd aged ten years in the last hour, looked set to come unglued with hysteria. Tough. She didn't feel anything for Haley but contempt.

She was worried about her own hide.

There seemed no way out.

She only prayed that Ki and Stone, one or the other or both, would show up and rain on whatever "party" Brutus had in mind.

Jessie looked through the iron bars of her cell. Up and down the cell block, grim, bearded, sweat-sheened faces were pressed up against the bars. In the wavering torchlight, the prisoners of Durango looked ghoulish, especially frightening to Jessie. They watched her, but they said nothing. And it was hotter in the cell block than it was outside, the air stifling, ripe with the stench of sweat and urine and feces. Sweat coursed down Jessie's face, stinging her eyes. Wiping her brow with the back of her hand, she kept searching her mind for some plan of attack, but couldn't come up with one, unless it was to somehow manage to grab one of her guns off Brutus . . . No, that was suicide.

"Why? Why is this happening?"

Jessie told Haley, "Maybe it's just like he said. Payback."

Haley looked confused, miserable. "I should've known better than to trust him. Man wanted by half the marshals in this country. It figures he was scheming to get his filthy hands on my gold and disappear into Mexico. I've been like a father to that man!"

"Funny you should mention something about fathers," Jessie said.

"What?" Haley peered at Jessie. "Why do I get this feeling I should know you, huh?"

Jessie sniffed with disgust and looked away from him. "Losing your gold, Haley, could end up proving to be the least of your worries. If it's up to me, that is."

Haley scowled at her. "Stop talking in goddam riddles, lady! I get the distinct feeling you rode into my town for some purpose, you and your friend. Who the hell are you?"

"In time, you might find out."

"You men, listen up!"

The voice of Brutus boomed through the iron-barred window. Jessie and Haley went to the window, squeezed close together to stare out into the courtyard. There, Brutus stood, hands on hips, grinning at the cell block.

"The party's about to begin, you men!" he went on. "Now, here's the deal. Depending on the amount of respect I get tonight, depending on your cooperation, I'll be setting you free in the morning. Any of you want to join me, you can, but you won't be getting a cut of any gold till you prove your worth to me. But there's still some decisions I need to make, so don't get all happy on me. Who knows what I'll do."

There was a lot of activity in the courtyard. And Jessie knew that a sick spectacle was about to get under way. Outlaws were dousing kerosene over the hot boxes that held the guards. Near the gallows, four outlaws with shovels were busy digging a hole in the ground, while two others hammered wooden planks together. Jessie saw rope and railroad spikes lying beside the wood. While they worked, outlaws drank from whiskey bottles, smoked cigars, chuckled among themselves.

"What's he going to do?" Haley breathed, eyes wide with fear. "He's sick, he's crazy! I can't believe this is happening. To me! I'm the richest man in the whole goddam Territory! This is a nightmare!"

"Now!" Brutus continued and began slowly pacing, back and forth, in front of the cell block. "Like I said, what this is about is respect. You see, the big man, Mr. Haley, I'm sure you've heard of him if you've heard of his town, well, he's keen on respect, but where he is now, well, it just goes to show that anything can happen in life and that all that glitters may not be gold. Why, freedom can glitter. See, a lot of you have had some bad breaks in life, maybe a lot of you are even innocent, so my heart goes out to you because if I weren't who I am,

150

well, shit, I could just as well be sitting where you are . . ."

"You're goddam right I'm innocent!" a prisoner wailed. "I didn't rape and kill any twelve-year-old girl. I like boys! They railroaded me!"

"Please!" Brutus roared. "Do not interrupt me. You've seen what can happen if I become upset. Now, what you're about to see happen here today, tonight, well, remember it. What I'm building is another monument to the legend of John Brutus."

The man was insane, Jessie thought. Stone-cold insane with the lust for power, money, and blood. He was like a rabid animal that needed to be put to sleep.

"Light me up a couple of those guards, fellas!" Brutus called over his shoulder. "I wanna hear 'em sing!"

Jessie watched as outlaws drenched two hot boxes with more kerosene, and the guards inside those boxes cried out in terror as it was poured through the air holes, soaking them. Matches were struck and tossed on the hot boxes. Instantly, a wall of flame roared over the boxes. Bone-chilling screams ripped from the fiery wall. Jessie turned away, unable to stomach the sight and sound of men being burned alive. She'd seen a lot of brutality in her day, and she was by no means squeamish, but this spectacle tore her apart with rage and a hunger for vengeance like she'd never known.

"Two more for an encore!" Brutus laughed. "Now, this is what I call respect for the law! The law of John Brutus, that is!"

The stench of roasting flesh wafted through the iron-barred window, assaulting Jessie's senses.

151

Haley dry-retched. Prisoners shouted encouragement.

Jessie looked back out the window, if for nothing else than to stoke her rage at the sight of the brutality and cold-blooded murder. She wanted all the incentive she could get, for when the time came, and it would she believed, she would wreak vengeance on Brutus and every outlaw there. She would fight fire with fire.

An outlaw put a bundle of dynamite in a pool of kerosene around one of the hot boxes. He slopped a trail of kerosene away from it and then repeated the same procedure with another box. He struck a match off his boot heel and lit both trails of flammable liquid. Tongues of fire blazed to life, racing for the hot boxes. Flames whooshed in a sudden roar over the boxes, the fuses on the dynamite sticks flared up, and then two ear-splitting explosions pulverized the hot boxes, hurling sections of iron and ragged hunks of wet, red meat into the air.

An outlaw shouted, "Yahooo! Look at 'em fly!" Then he stuck a cigar into the fiery hell consuming the other two guards, who were no longer screaming in agony, and lit the end of his stogie.

"Okay. The show must go on." Brutus laughed. "Now, I've heard about your fine warden, Bob Teetleman."

"He's a piece of shit! He treats us worse than animals! You gonna do 'im, do 'im slow!"

"I gotcha," Brutus said. "I hear your plea. Now. What I've heard about old Bob, well, I understand he's a religious man."

"Uppity son of a bitch!" a prisoner snarled. "You got that right, big man. Always readin' the Bible at us. Tellin' us we ain't even fit for Hell."

"Okay, okay." Brutus held up a hand. "I've seen plenty of guys all over the Territory just like Bob. Even know of a preacher back in the old man's town who's now a pimp. He'll screw and suck anything with a gash between the legs while telling you you've got to repent of your sins. Strange world we live in, fellas. Is it ready?" Brutus yelled over his shoulder.

An outlaw barked, "Yeah." And then four of them lifted the wood planks they had hammered and roped together.

Jessie felt her breath catch in her throat, her heart pounding in her ears as she saw the cross stood up by the outlaws. She knew what was coming next.

Brutus confirmed her suspicions. "Hey now, better lay it back down till we get somebody on it." They dropped the cross. "You men," he told the prisoners, "since Bob's such a fine upstanding religious man, I'm gonna let you call it. What do you want seen done to him?" Heavy silence, followed as Brutus gestured mockingly, placing his hand over his ear as if urging the prisoners to reply. "What was that? I hear you say, 'Crucify him.' C'mon, boys, all the Bible Bob preaches at ya, you should know what happened to Jesus. Let me hear it."

"Awright, crucify him!" a prisoner called.

"What was that!?" Brutus laughed. "I can't hear you!"

"Crucify him!" another prisoner shouted.

"Louder!"

"Crucify him, yeah, give the old bastard a taste of his own bullshit!"

"Crucify him . . . Crucify him!"

Other prisoners joined in the chant, until the whole courtyard was ringing with *"Crucify... Crucify him..."*

"Nail his ass up!"

Haley muttered an oath. Jessie watched as outlaws hauled the warden out of the hot box while the insane chant roared on. Teetleman struggled as he was led to the cross.

"No!" the warden screamed, as he was forced down on the cross, his arms and legs lashed with rope to the wood. An outlaw picked up a hammer and a railroad spike.

"Noooo!!!"

Brutus gestured mockingly as if washing his hands.

The hammer came down.

Bone crunched and Teetleman shrieked.

Chapter 13

Long, dark shadows were beginning to stretch over the courtyard of Durango.

Beyond the window of her cell, Jessie saw the sun setting to the west, a huge fiery red eye that seemed to sit almost on top of the black prison wall. Outlaws, swigging whiskey and talking in low-voiced conversations, roamed around the slaughterbed. A buzzard had perched itself on the pinnacle of the cross that held Warden Teetleman, while the ominous black shapes of other vultures circled the prison above.

It was a vulture feast out there, and all the scavenger birds had to do, Jessie thought, was wait for the damned to consume one another.

Teetleman was now dead, had been shot about an hour ago by Brutus. The warden hung there, nailed on his cross, facing the cell block. Fires around the hot boxes, and the wreckage of the boxes that had been blown up by dynamite, had died down to small tongues of crackling flame. Brutus had put the torch to the other boxes, burning to death the remainder of the guards. Horses could still be heard whickering in short outbursts of panic, as the stink of death, the stench of burning flesh, filled the courtyard. There had been no sign of Brutus since he'd disappeared into the warden's quarters after shooting Teetleman once in the chest, putting the final silence to the warden's groans of agony.

And Jessie felt as if she were waiting for her own death sentence. She told herself to hang on, believe, there would be a way out. She was determined not to become something for the buzzards to feed on. Somehow, she was going to break herself free.

Haley was sitting on the edge of the cot. For a man who had seemed so tough and in control yesterday, Haley looked completely defeated to Jessie—small, weak, and cowardly. He hadn't moved in quite a while; he just sat there in sullen silence. The sight of Haley disgusted her. The least he could do, she figured, was die like a man. But, she knew, having personally witnessed it time and again, bad men can't do that, can't die with bravery or grace or dignity; they can't accept death because they fear it far, far worse than someone who's lived or tried to live a good life. They'll fight to hold onto the last breath in a suicidal rage, or they'll plead and snivel to be spared when it comes their time to die, even though they themselves never showed mercy or spared a life they held in their hands. The more she looked at Haley, the more he revolted her. She shook her head to herself. This was the same man who had only yesterday claimed he could hold his own. Brutus had made the king naked.

Some excited low-voiced conversations rippled up and down the cell block, as prisoners chatted among themselves about the possibility of being free men. But Jessie knew Brutus intended to kill every prisoner there. He was as evil as any man she'd ever come across. Death would be too good, she thought, for John Brutus.

Suddenly she spotted the big shape of the outlaw leader as he came out of the warden's quarters and walked across the courtyard. He barked orders at several of his men, who picked up buckets of kerosene and bundles of dynamite and followed him toward the cell block.

Jessie tensed, as moments later Brutus's big shadow filled the corridor beyond her cell.

"You lettin' us out, John?"

"C'mon, John, we'll ride with ya, we're good men!"

"Everybody quiet down!" Brutus growled. Within a minute, outlaws were sloshing kerosene up and down the floor of the cell block and setting bundles of dynamite out in the middle of the floor. Prisoners cursed, demanded to know what was going on. "Shut up, allaya! Keep it up, I'll torch the whole goddam place right now!"

"He's gonna fry us all!" a prisoner screamed. "He's gonna blow us up clear into the sky!"

"Shoot that man!" Brutus ordered, and, a moment later, gunfire rang out.

A body thudded to the floor.

Grim silence filled the cell block after the echo of the killing shot died.

Haley rushed the cell door and grabbed the bars, his face twisted with rage. "You let me outta here, now! You can't do this to me, you can't treat me like this! I'm somebody important. I'll have you hunted down like a dog and shot!"

Brutus laughed. "You ain't gonna do shit, Max. You ain't nobody, Max, that's some of the point to this. Now. When the sun goes down, I'm gonna show you just what a nobody you are."

"What do you mean?"

"I mean, Max, I'm going to hang you. Hey, cheer up, least I'm givin' you a little while to make your peace."

Haley's face went ashen with fear. "N-no . . . no. What do you want? John, tell me. I'll give you anything, more gold, take the woman here."

Brutus roared with laughter. "I'm taking the woman anyway, Max. See, that's the final slap in the face. While you're swinging by the neck, I'll be doing some swinging of my own. And Jessie there, she'll decide if she wants to ride to Mexico with me. Or spend her last moments on earth in a cell full of men who ain't had a woman in some time. 'Course, I got a little plan before I ride out of here. This whole place is gonna burn. Life is beautiful when you're winning, ain't it, Max?"

As Brutus stood there, laughing in Haley's face, Jessie burned with silent rage. The eyes of John Brutus seemed to glow with his madness. For a moment, Jessie was amazed, thinking back on how cool Brutus had appeared in Haley. And all the time he had known full well what he was going to do here. He'd worn the mask of a devil, a liar.

Finally, Brutus wheeled and left the cell block.

"No," Haley sputtered and moved back to his cot on wooden legs. "How can it be?"

Jessie looked out the window. "Ki," she muttered. "Where are you?"

Their horses tethered to brush out on the plateau, Ki, Stone, and Christine crept toward the edge of the rise.

They had arrived, but what was awaiting them? Ki wondered. All day they had ridden in hard silence. A day that had dragged by like an eternity to Ki, as he worried and feared for Jessie.

And catching the whiff of burning flesh in the hot air, as the sun sank beyond the hills to the west, Ki feared the worst.

He crouched and put a hand on Christine's shoulder, and she dropped to a knee.

"Good . . . Lord," Christine breathed in horror.

And Ki stared down into the prison courtyard. He saw the signs of death, the cross with its crucified victim. He counted maybe three dozen outlaws wandering around the courtyard, all of them armed to the teeth. He feared for Jessie, his blood boiling with rage, his heart pounding. He sniffed the air, pungent with the stench of kerosene, ripe with the stink of death. What had happened down there? Was Jessie even still alive? There was some wreckage against the west wall and several bodies strewn around the courtyard. Had all the guards been killed? Had Haley and Brutus taken over the prison? Why?

Stone looked at Ki. "Well. They're down there. Don't ask me what the hell it is we're seeing. I don't see any sign of Jessie . . ."

"But there's only one way to find out if she's there," Ki finished. He searched the hills to the south.

"Stone, we'll make our way around the plateau. There's only one guard tower, and I don't see anybody watching from there. Looks to me like Brutus and his pack, they've taken over the prison. The way they're walking around down there, they think they're untouchable. Once we're on the other side, in those hills, we'll come down and make our way through the front gate. It'll be dark soon; we'll move in under the cover of night. There's no other way in I can see, except that one opening. And there's only one way to do this, Stone, one way in, one way out."

A grim smile cut Stone's battered face. "I like the way you think, Ki. We'll take down the prison just like we did Haley. Walk in there and cut down anything that moves."

"Anything that is, but Jessie. Let's go," he said, and led Stone and Christine back to their mounts.

"I could've built an empire, I could've had it all. No, I had it all."

Jessie looked away from Haley. Night had fallen over the prison. Firelight wavered through the bars of their window, as Jessie went to the window and saw outlaws moving around the courtyard with torches in hand. They were splashing kerosene up and down the length of the base of the cell-block wall, laying bundles of dynamite down in the pools of kerosene. A good number of them were drunk on whiskey. Brutus was hell-bent on blowing up the whole prison, burning it to ashes and dust.

Haley sniffed the air. "What are they doing?"

Jessie ignored him.

Outlaws doused the hanging body of Teetleman with kerosene, then put the torch to the crucified corpse. From out of the flickering firelight, Brutus appeared and strode for the cell block.

It was hanging time for Max Haley, Jessie knew. She had to get Brutus's gun; she had to do something to save herself . . . Brutus cheating her of her vengeance on Haley was now the least of her worries.

Moments later, surrounded by a dozen outlaws, Brutus unlocked the cell door and told Haley, "It's time to go, Max. Any last words?"

Haley shook his head and cried, "No. Don't do it!"

"Watch her close. She moves, shoot her!" Brutus ordered, then walked into the cell and grabbed Haley by his shirtfront, hauling him, blubbering and pleading for his life, out into the corridor.

Unwavering rifles and revolvers trained on her, Jessie stepped out into the corridor. Once she was outside, she'd have to make her move—grab a gun, start blasting away, seek cover, and move the hell on out of the prison.

"Why?" Haley cried, as Brutus kicked him in the ass and sent him stumbling out into the courtyard. "Why are you doing this? It doesn't make any sense! We've got it all, we've got a town, we've got money!"

"No, I got it all, Max," Brutus chuckled. "And, damn, c'mon, you're embarrassing me. Why don't you just go on and die like a man. I look at Jessie here; she looks disgusted with the sight of all this sniveling you're doing. Goddam. You of all people, Max, you should understand. It's about power. It's about being top dog."

Jessie saw two outlaws, up on the gallows, standing next to the noose.

The maddening buzz of flies filled the air.

Flames crackled.

A lone buzzard spread its wings, a dark shadowy thing lifting itself above the wavering glow of firelight.

Horses whinnied.

From behind her, Jessie heard the soft whimpering of a prisoner crying, "He's gonna kill us all. I don't deserve to die like this . . ."

Jessie was led to the gallows, then made to stop beside the hangman's stage. Through a narrowed gaze, she checked the outlaws standing beside her. One was standing about six feet away from her, as if he were afraid to get too close to her. The other one stood less than three feet from her, holding a torch in one hand, a Winchester rifle in the other. He had a bundle of dynamite jammed through his holster, and he was puffing on a cigar as if he didn't have a care in the world. She looked away from the butt of his holstered Colt just as the outlaw turned to grin at her.

Ki didn't know what was happening down in the prison courtyard or why, but he spotted Jessie near the gallows. They had put the torch to the victim on the cross, and the air was rife with the sickly sweet stink of burning flesh. Ki, Stone, and Christine were crouched now in a gulley just south of the prison. From their high vantage point they could see everything that was happening in the courtyard. Someone was being shoved toward the foot of the gallows. That shadow's voice cried out, "No, John, don't do this!"

"Haley," Stone said, looking puzzled, Winchester rifle in hand. "Looks like Brutus has taken over the show. But why?"

"Well, if it's the town he wants, he won't be riding back to anything but a pile of ashes," Ki said. "The dream is dead. Now let's give him the full treatment of a nightmare."

It had taken some time, longer than Ki wanted, but they'd made their way to the south hills. Softly, Ki cursed, knowing it would take a few critical minutes to scurry down the gulley and make their way up the east wall.

"Christine, you stay here," Ki ordered the girl. "Do not move, do not come down. No matter what happens."

"Ki, what happens if . . . I can't even say it."

Ki looked at Christine, hard-eyed. He nodded at Stone, who handed Christine the spare Colt. "Then you ride and don't look back."

"There's a stash of money down there," Stone said. "That's the only reason I can think of for Brutus turning on his boss."

"Money's the least of my worries now, Stone. Come on," Ki growled over his shoulder, Colt in hand.

Quickly, Ki, trailed by Stone, melted into the night. He reached the foot of the hills and advanced on the wall of the prison.

Silently, *ninja*-style, he crept up the length of the east wall. At least, he thought, Jessie was still alive. He had a vest full of *shurikens*, his sword, and his holstered Colt. Time to deal out a nightmare, he thought.

Jessie tensed to make her move.

Two outlaws kicked and pushed Haley up the steps of the gallows.

Sweat burned into Jessie's eyes, and her heart raced. Only a miracle would get her out of this, she knew. Or only sheer daring, pure guts.

Finally, they got Haley onto the gallows and slipped the noose over his head. He clawed at the noose as an outlaw tugged it tight around his neck, then rested his hand on the lever to the trapdoor.

"Not so fast," Brutus called up the gallows, and the outlaw removed his hand from the lever. "Don't bother roping his hands or feet. I wanna see him dance when he falls. Okay, I want everybody to join me in a moment of prayer for Max Haley." A second later, Brutus laughed. "Yeah, right."

The outlaw pack roared with laughter.

Jessie drew a deep breath and steeled herself to grab the revolver from the holster of the outlaw beside her. And if she could grab the dynamite, light the fuse with his cigar . . .

Then her miracle happened.

Gunshots rolled over the courtyard. Jessie saw two outlaws, blood spurting away from their chests, pitch to the ground.

She glimpsed the shadows surging past the gate opening, a rifle and a revolver flaming pinpoints stabbing through the gloom.

Ki and Stone.

Jessie clawed free the Colt from the holster of the outlaw beside her as hell descended over the prison.

Chapter 14

There was an execution, all right. In fact, there were nothing but executions.

But it was Jessie, Ki, and a man named Stone who became the executioners. And in the blink of an eye the trio descended on the Brutus gang with all the rampaging fury of a buffalo stampede, with a hellstorm of lead death and steel vengeance that seemed to drop over the outlaws from straight out of the black sky of night.

Jessie slid the Colt revolver from the outlaw's holster, as the gunman's cigar fell from his lips, startled as he was by the sudden weapons fire blazing across the courtyard. Jessie pumped a bullet into the man's ear. As the slug shot out the other side of his skull, cleaving away a chunk of bone and flinging his hat through the air behind a pink-gray mist of blood and brains, Jessie wheeled and drilled the other outlaw flanking her square in the chest, kicking him onto his back, his face etched in shock and horror for all eternity. Two down, she saw, but too many to go. She was grimly aware that she'd need all her lethal skill and relentless determination, plus a little luck, to fight her way out of the ensuing slaughter. The dynamite, she knew, could turn the tide of battle in their favor.

Outlaws, some drunk on whiskey, others paralyzed for critical moments by fear, began dropping like flies as the shadows that were Ki and Stone surged across the courtyard, steel flying, guns blazing.

Ki hurled a *shuriken*, a silver blur twirling through the firelight that glowed off Teetleman's cross. Then Jessie's bodyguard began triggering his Colt like there was no tomorrow.

His battered face cut with savage determination, Stone repeatedly jacked the lever action on his Winchester, the rifle's muzzle flaming again and again, piercing the Stygian gloom, lead fingers of death stabbing into the backs and skulls and necks of outlaws scrambling for holstered iron. Outlaw blood jetted through the air, and bodies pitched to the already crimson-soaked earth, to lie there twitching, and later become a gory buzzard feast.

Not wasting a split second, glimpsing the steel star embedded in the throat of an outlaw who jerked and twitched and dropped beneath a spurting geyser of blood arcing from his severed jugular, Jessie plucked the dynamite bundle off his body, scooped up his cigar, lit the fuse, and tossed the hellpack through the night. Despite the murderous chaos around her, as she darted away from the frenzied swirl of outlaws scurrying to return fire on their attackers, Jessie kept a grim eye on the hangman's stage. She wanted Haley all for herself, but Max Haley, she feared, and silently cursed, was in danger of dying in the cross fire or plummeting through the trapdoor by accident.

The dynamite bundle, fuse sizzling down to the final half inch, bounced and rolled up in the dust bowl blowing through outlaws tripping over one another in their haste to fight back.

Vile curses, panic-edged shouts, ripped the night.

Ki and Stone, splitting up, advanced on the outlaw pack and kept on firing for all they were worth. Together they proved themselves worth plenty.

Behind the carnage, the prisoners roared with fear and panic, an uproar of terror mixed with grim hope, booming from the cell block and seeming to shake the dark walls of Durango and send black-winged scavenger demons wheeling for the sky.

An outlaw, eyes wide with terror, looked at the dynamite pack rolling up between his legs. He took a running step, screaming, "Dynamite!"

Then the dynamite bundle blew, creating a huge ball of fire that catapulted more than a dozen outlaws, and various dismembered parts, through the air. A tidal wave of dust and grit, a flying wall of rocks and severed limbs, bowled down many surviving outlaws. And the explosive earthquakelike tremor of the blast knocked several other outlaws off their feet. Enraged, John Brutus picked himself up off the ground and bellowed with fury, his face streaked with blood from scissoring bits of stone shrapnel.

The cries of wounded men in agony lanced the air.

Jessie raced for the back of the gallows, her Colt barking twice and tearing open the chests of two outlaws, sending them spinning and crashing into each other. Up on the gallows, gunfire was flaming her way. She hit the ground, rolling, as bullets whined in a tracking path behind her. On her belly, she looked up and cracked a round from her Colt that smashed into the face of one of Brutus's would-be hangmen. The lethal shot caved the outlaw's face in and launched him off the gallows, his dead weight splintering the railing as he plunged for the ground. As the din of weapons fire rattled the night, Jessie saw a line of slugs march up the stomach and chest of the other outlaw hangman, who spun and just missed slamming into the lever that would release the trapdoor. He crumpled up at the feet of Haley. Ki and Stone were continuing their hell march, Jessie saw, dark shadows rolling across the courtyard, guns flaming and spitting lead, creating an orgy of death around the gallows. She would need all the help she could get, Jessie knew.

And she focused her mind and will on vengeance. A wall of dust swept over her, as limbs thudded to the ground around her. Haley was slipping the noose off his neck.

Horses bucked and whinnied in panic near the warden's quarters, and began tearing their reins free from the railing to flee the slaughter.

Jessie shadowed beneath the trapdoor of the gallows, checking her rear and flanks for any sign of gunmen, but Ki and Stone were dropping outlaws all around her, covering her tracks with deadly gunfire. Haley was all hers, she thought, unless a wild shot killed him. She was determined not to let that happen as she raced for the foot of the gallows.

• • •

Jessie was a mere shadow to Ki in the roaring bands of firelight rolling over him, but he saw she was safe for the moment. Quickly, angling behind the horses racing across the courtyard, he reloaded his Colt.

The fight, he knew, was far from over. Even as Ki reloaded, bullets thudded into animal flesh around him, and horses plummeted to the earth. He moved on sideways, seeking cover behind other racing mounts.

Suddenly, its wood eaten away by fire, the flaming cross toppled, crushing two outlaws beneath it. A shower of sparks, an explosion of fiery bark and dust, billowed over the scene. And one outlaw began shrieking like a banshee as flames ignited him into a human torch that whirled and ran across the courtyard, arms engulfed in fire and slapping at his face and head.

Ki darted between two fleeing mounts, surging into the wall of dust kicked up by thundering hooves. Ahead, beyond the smoking, shriveled black mummy that had pitched facedown in the bed of flames, Ki saw John Brutus. Outlined in the firelight, he was dragging one of his men along, his arm wrapped around the outlaw's throat as he used him like a shield to beat a hasty retreat from the killing area around the gallows and begin skirting down the length of the cell-block face. The human shield Brutus was using was clawing at his face, but it was a halfhearted effort since the outlaw in Brutus's deathhold was covered in blood, half of his leg having been blown away by the explosion. The stump was pumping blood everywhere and quickly draining the life out of that hapless, mangled outlaw.

Ki drew a bead on Brutus.

"He's mine, Ki!"

Startled, Ki found Stone on his left flank.

"He murdered my wife!" Stone shouted at Ki through the din of weapons fire, the crackling of fire, and the pounding of hooves. "Brutus is mine!"

Ki nodded and moved on for the gallows, hell-bent on covering Jessie's back as the heiress hit the gallows steps. All right, Ki decided, Stone could have Brutus, provided, of course, the outlaw didn't suddenly start firing on Jessie.

It became obvious that Brutus had a terrible plan to cover his retreat, as he flung his human shield to the ground and scooped up a discarded torch near a bullet-riddled, dynamite-shredded corpse. On a dead run, Brutus hurled the torch toward the cell block.

"Nooooo!!!" a prisoner screamed, as the torch hit the base of the wall.

Ki could only watch, drilling an outlaw in the chest, his Colt blazing, as the front of the cell-block wall whooshed into a brilliant, rolling wall of fire. Seconds later, explosions began peppering the cell block. Tortured screams pierced the night, and Ki realized that Brutus had rigged the whole block with dynamite, intending to take the whole place down behind him. *Or with him!* The big outlaw was insane, Ki thought as huge slabs of debris were vomited into the air, riding shooting tongues of roaring fire. The concussive series of blasts, the showering chunks of stone and body parts, hammered outlaws to the ground. Within seconds, a fiery mountain loomed over the cell block and more blasts rocked the prison compound. The explosions covered Brutus's flight across the courtyard.

A blinding flash ripped across Jessie's grim vision. One explosion after another from the dynamite inside the cell block shattered the night with ear-piercing detonations. Giant, razoring hunks of debris washed over the gallows, slamming into its base and threatening to uproot the whole structure. Jessie ducked, bits and pieces of stone slapping into her body, her ears ringing from the brutal noise of explosions, from the bone-chilling wails of men dying in terrible pain, either being burned alive or scythed apart by dynamite blasts. When she looked up, she spotted Haley at the top of the steps. His face was twisted by maniacal rage, and there was a revolver in his hand.

"You bitch, say good night!" Haley shouted. "You had your chance, God damn you to Hell!"

Then a slab of raining stone pelted Haley, knocking him off-balance, his gun roaring, the slug whining off the railing beside Jessie.

Crouched, surging up the steps, Jessie flinched as bullets began peppering her right flank. She pivoted and spotted Hanks charging the gallows from the gloom, the one-eyed gunman fanning the hammer of his Colt. She shot him in the stomach with cool, lethal precision, and then Hanks's shirtfront exploded in crimson, fist-sized holes. Jessie took a split second to glimpse Ki pounding Hanks's back with a savage lead barrage that hurled him forward like a rag doll.

Haley wobbled to his feet.

Jessie hit the top of the steps, just as Haley swung his revolver her way. Another explosion rocked the prison compound, threw Jessie's aim off a hair, and she shot Haley in the leg. He screamed.

Ki went berserk with final, terrible vengeance, unsheathing his sword. Steel flashing, he lopped heads and skewered outlaws, while his Colt flamed and pumped killing rounds into masks of rage and hate. As bodies pitched all around him, Ki surged on.

"Bitch!" Haley screamed.

Jessie bounded onto the gallows.

Haley scrambled for his Colt, tried to stand. As he teetered, began to fall sideways, Jessie kicked the revolver out of his hand. In one lightning motion, she slipped the noose around Haley's neck. She pulled the rope so tight that Haley's eyes bulged, both in pain and in horror.

Explosions puked apart both the lower and upper cell-block tiers in one long, ceaseless stream of vomiting fireballs, converging mountains of fire and smoke lifting wreckage and men skyward, scattering black clouds of vultures above the prison.

"Who are you!?" Haley shouted, clawing at the rope cutting into his neck.

"I'm the daughter of Alex Starbuck," Jessie told Haley in a cold voice.

Haley froze, his jaw agape. "Alex . . . Starbuck. He . . ."

"Right. My father was murdered. You were named by him as someone who was part of an organization responsible for killing him."

Haley shook his head.

Jessie pushed the lever and released the trapdoor.

"Nooo . . ."

Haley's scream was cut off as he dropped through the trapdoor, his twisted mask of rage and terror, his bulging eyes, staring up through the opening at Jessie. A moment later, there was the sound of a neck snapping as the rope jerked taut.

And Max Haley stared at nothing.

Adrenaline racing through her, Jessie scooped up a discarded revolver and hit the bottom of the steps. Behind her, Haley swung by the neck.

Ki shadowed up beside Jessie.

A delayed explosion ripped apart the night.

Jessie looked at Ki and showed her bodyguard a grim smile. "Ki, I was wondering when you'd get here."

"Believe me, Jessie, I was beginning to wonder if I'd ever get here myself. Good to see you alive and unhurt."

"Likewise to you, my friend."

The stench of burning flesh in her nose, Jessie searched the grounds for any sign of life.

There was nothing but death.

But a wounded outlaw arose from the slaughterbed. His Colt drew a bead on Jessie.

"Look out!" Ki shouted, shouldering into Jessie, knocking her sideways as the bullet cracked from the outlaw's revolver and whined off the ground where a split second before Jessie had been standing. Together, Jessie and Ki buried that outlaw beneath a quick barrage of lead.

Hard-eyed and grim-faced, the two of them fanned the slaughterbed with their weapons poised to fire. They found nothing but twitching limbs, burning flesh. They checked the front of the cell block. Nothing moved behind the thick, swirling walls of black smoke and crackling tongues of fire.

Jessie couldn't believe anything could have lived through the series of explosions that had uprooted the entire cell block.

Moments later, as she listened to the crackle of fire all around her and smelled the stench of roasting flesh, she knew that, indeed, no prisoner had lived through that explosive and hellish bonfire.

"Stone!" Jessie breathed, then searched the court-yard.

Two shadows were moving through the gloom, outlined for a moment by leaping fire. Brutus, Jessie saw, was running for the prisoner-transport wagon with its gold cargo.

Stone was loping after Brutus.

"Come on, Ki!"

"He said Brutus murdered his wife!"

"He told you right," Jessie answered.

"Brutus!" Stone shouted, jacking the lever action on his Winchester.

Startled, Brutus whirled, revolver in hand.

A shot rang out.

Brutus screamed, clutched his leg as blood spurted away from his thigh, and toppled into the side of the transport wagon.

Jessie closed on Stone's side.

Stone unleathered his Remington.

Ki watched Jessie's back for any signs of other possums. Nothing moved from the sea of bodies behind them.

In the ensuing silence, as Brutus struggled to stand, the flames seemed to grow angrier, stronger.

"You took away from me the only thing I ever loved in this world," Stone growled.

"Ain't that just too fuckin' bad!" Brutus rasped through clenched teeth.

The revolver in his trembling hand came up and swung toward Stone.

And Stone pinned Brutus to the side of the wagon with a shot through the outlaw's upper chest. With one slow forward step after another, Stone kept pumping lead into Brutus.

Fire roared.

Stone walked on, fired.

Brutus twitched, blood spraying over his face.

The Remington barked again in Stone's hand.

Brutus screamed in rage and pain.

Jessie watched through a cold, slit-eyed gaze.

Ki holstered his Colt.

Stone's final shot drilled through Brutus's forehead.

The back of the outlaw's head hammered into the wagon. Then, slowly, he toppled forward.

Buzzard meat.

Chapter 15

Minutes after the final killing shot echoed across the courtyard, several buzzards floated down through the clouds of black smoke rising above the slaughter. The big, shadowy winged shapes of dozens of other vultures now choked the air above Durango.

Christine ran through the gate opening, gun in hand, and cried out, "Ki!"

Jessie spotted her, looked at Ki, and smiled.

"You wouldn't believe what I've gone through for that girl," Ki told Jessie.

"Oh, I'd believe it. What did I hear you tell her before? That you're something of a romantic?"

Ki chuckled and moved away from Jessie. "You make it sound like I could have put my foot in my mouth, Jessie."

"Wouldn't be the first time," she called after Ki in good-natured humor.

Then Jessie retrieved her weapons off the body of Brutus. She stood beside Stone.

Stone smiled at her and put a gentle hand on her face. "I'm damn glad you're alive, Jessie. The world would be a little sadder and emptier place tomorrow if you weren't in it."

"I'm glad you're alive, too, Stone. And thanks for coming here with Ki. Thanks for caring."

"I wouldn't have had it any other way."

She held Stone's smile for a moment, then moved to pluck a key off Brutus's gunbelt and hand it to Stone.

"What's this?"

"Open one of those trunks inside the wagon," she answered.

Stone did. And when he saw the gold, glittering before him in the outreaching fingers of firelight, he let out a soft whistle.

"All of them?" he asked.

"Every one of them. Haley said there was a quarter million dollars' worth of gold there."

A warm smile reached from Stone's lips to brighten his eyes. "Well, I guess I won't need to be dragging my bounty all over the desert, after all. Looks like Mr. Haley's gold just saved that orphanage I told you about. And then some."

"I'm happy for you, Stone. Something good comes out of all this bad."

"What about you?"

"What about me?"

"Well, we could split this up."

"No." Jessie shook her head. "You see, Joe, I've got all the money I'll ever need, and even if I didn't, those kids in the orphanage need it a lot more than I do."

Joe peered at Jessie. "Just who are you?"

"Why, I'm a wealthy heiress, Joe. My last name's Starbuck."

Stone let loose with another soft whistle. "Yeah, I've heard the name. I've also heard something about the Lone Star legend. I'll be damned. That's you and Ki."

Jessie nodded.

Stone kissed Jessie tenderly, then pulled back, staring deep into her green eyes for a long moment. "You don't even have to say it, Jessie. I know. It's time for us to part."

"For now. Maybe if I get out to San Francisco, I'll look you up."

"Saint Joseph's, that's the orphanage. You get out that way, you look me up, or I'll be mighty sore. No maybes about it."

Jessie kissed Stone. "I'll miss you, Joe Stone. We'll meet again, believe me. I'll look forward to it."

Stone looked past Jessie and nodded at Christine as the girl ran up to Ki and threw herself in his arms. "I'll, uh, I'll take the girl with me. She'll be safe. Ki doesn't strike me as the type to, uh . . . well, I don't know quite how to put it . . ."

"He's not. We travel alone. It's better that way. For one thing, no innocents will get hurt. Christine is definitely an innocent, despite what she might think of herself."

Ki told Christine as much. She didn't like it, but she saw something in Ki's face that made her accept the moment of parting. A silent tear rolled down her cheek as she hugged and kissed him.

"You even gonna miss me a little?" Christine asked.

"No. I'm going to miss you a lot."

Ki and Christine spent a few moments talking, and Jessie told Christine she would be safe with Stone. Christine reluctantly agreed to go with Stone and start a new life for herself in San Francisco. Stone promised her enough gold to make a good start for herself in the big city.

With a *shuriken*, Ki left the Lone Star trademark of vengeance, the steel star spearing into the wooden beam of the gallows.

The man who would be king of the Arizona Territory swayed in the stinking breeze of death.

The crackling of raging flames swirled around Jessie and Ki.

It was time to leave that place of death and horror.

Chapter 16

It was around mid-morning the day after the slaughter at Durango when Jessie and Ki spotted them in the distance.

The heiress and her bodyguard, their mounts having been watered and well fed back at the prison trough, were moving northwest across the barren plain that was once again baking under a fiery sun.

Destination: Tempest. Goal: a long rest at the Circle Star Ranch.

Far, far behind Jessie and Ki, the blue sky was smudged black in spots with tiny puffs of drifting smoke.

Late last night, they had parted from Stone and Christine. It was a bittersweet farewell, and, yes, Jessie knew she'd miss the man named Stone. Likewise, judging by Ki's somber silence, the wistful look in his almond eyes, she figured Ki was having lingering good thoughts about Christine.

But the moment demanded vigilance.

Tension building inside of her, Jessie stared ahead.

And she counted fifteen figures on horseback, slowly riding through the shimmering heat waves rising off the burning desert floor.

Jessie looked at Ki. His face was hard and covered in sweat, sword by his side, Colt in his holster.

"I forgot to tell you something," Jessie said. Quickly, she told Ki about the governor of the Territory, the marshals, and the politicians from back east who were to meet up with Haley at Durango to receive their payoff.

Ki just smiled. "Well, we'll finish it like we started it. By ear. Let them call it. Maybe they'll just ride on by."

As they closed the gap between them and the shimmering apparitions, Jessie saw the sunlight winking off steel stars pinned to about ten chests.

Easing out of the rippling heat curtains, the riders from the north reined in their mounts. They weren't about to go around the lone woman and her companion.

Jessie and Ki stopped, a dozen feet right in front of the riders.

They were the law, Jessie knew, but they were also the lawless. Maybe not today, but maybe tomorrow, they would get theirs, she thought.

Fifteen pairs of hard eyes beneath black Stetsons scoured the lone woman and her companion. Flies buzzed, picked at sweat running down grim, clean-shaven faces.

The silence stretched.

Jessie's stare wandered over the butts of Colt Peacemakers, the stocks of Winchester rifles.

A horse whickered, its tail lashing at a swarm of flies circling its lathered flanks.

A portly man with white sideburns, dressed in a suit and tie, and looking uncomfortable in the saddle, nodded at Jessie, touched the brim of his derby, and said, "Ma'am. Good day to you. Men, let's ride on."

They moved out, slowly easing around Jessie and Ki.

Jessie urged her mount ahead. She looked at Ki, who held her grim stare.

They chanced a look behind. One of the marshals was twisted around in his saddle. He watched Jessie and Ki through a narrowed gaze, as the gap between the parties widened. Jessie sensed the lawman's suspicion. But he finally turned around in the saddle and looked straight ahead.

Jessie showed Ki a half grin.

"Won't they be surprised," he said in a low, tight-lipped voice.

"Remind me to send the governor an anonymous wire. Tell him his payoff went for a good cause. I hope he likes children."

Watch for

LONE STAR AND THE GOLD MINE

128th novel in the exciting LONE STAR series
from Jove

Coming in April!

WESTERNS!

NO OBLIGATION

Mail the coupon below

To start your subscription and receive 2 FREE WESTERNS, fill out the coupon below and mail it today. We'll send your first shipment which includes 2 FREE BOOKS as soon as we receive it.

From the Creators of Longarm!

Featuring the beautiful Jessica Starbuck and her loyal half-American half-Japanese martial arts sidekick Ki.